A KING ASCENDS

A KING ASCENDS:
Book One of the Tyrea Trilogy

Copyright © 2022 by Jane McKay
All rights reserved.

This is a work of fiction. Names characters, places, and incidents are the product of the author's imagination or are used fictitiously. Any similarity to actual persons, living or dead, events, or locations is entirely coincidental.

ISBN: 978-1-7379427-0-2 (Paperback Edition)
ISBN: 978-1-7379427-1-9 (eBook Edition)

Cover Design: SelfPubCovers.com/billwyc

No part of this publication may be reproduced or stored in a retrieval system, or transmitted in any form, or by any means of electronic, mechanical, photocopying, recording, or otherwise, without the written permission of the author or publisher.

Printed in the United States of America.
Published by arrangement with IngramSpark.
www.ingramspark.com

Also by Jane McKay
Available from Amazon and other retailers

The Tyrea Trilogy:
A King Ascends: Book One

Young Adult Novels

The Pebble Trilogy:
Pebble, Adventure of a Drone: Book One
To Look to a Star: Book Two *(coming soon)*

A KING ASCENDS

By

Jane McKay

Dedicated to:

All the men and women out there,
Who fight the good fight,
Against life takers—small and large.

Soldiers
Fire Personnel
Police Personnel
Teachers
Clergy
Case Workers
Judges
Politicians
Medical Personnel

"Fas est ab hoste doceri.
One should learn even from one's enemies."

—Ovid, Metamorphoses

CHAPTER 1

*B*lack mists swirled around his thoughts, keeping them unclear, always just out of reach. Urgency surged through him. There was something he needed to do. He tried to focus on the thought, but it receded into the distance.

"Come on, respond dammit! What the…?"

The doctor snatched her hands from the hot flesh as she reacted to the sudden golden aura pulsing from the patient's body. Red blood infused the skin as a white film developed, forming a protective shell.

"What is that?" a nurse exclaimed.

All of the monitors in the room screeched warnings, causing the medical team to jump. The noise increased, and medical personnel bumped equipment, backing away from the figure prone in the center of the room.

"Doctor, he's flat-lined!" the nurse shouted. The team moved into rapid but controlled action. Here was something they all understood. The frantic movements became focused and smooth. Each knew their job, performing around each other in the particular dance of health professionals. The shiny white emergency room reflected the tense drama being played out within its walls. The twelve-foot square space suddenly seemed much smaller as people maneuvered for position. The emergency room, usually cool, seemed to increase in temperature in response to the frantic activity.

The glow of the patient's skin faded, the alarms stopped, and everyone gave a sigh of relief. The quiet monitors resumed recording again, showing them within normal human limits—or what she hoped were his normal limits. Now the calm beeps seemed abnormally loud in the room. The medical team stared at the monitors, then at each other. They had handled the emergency according to standard procedure.

The only prison hospital on the planet, Greenwich, the staff handled both local patients and inmates from fifty different worlds due to the lack of other nearby medical facilities. Each patient had slightly unique physiology because of differences in gravity and climate.

They could hear the quiet rush as other doctors and medical personnel worked in nearby rooms on the other patients brought in with this one. None had life-threatening injuries, just a collection of broken bones or concussions. None had exhibited the amazing ability to form protective shields over their injuries.

A planetary shuttle crashing close to the prison was highly unusual on their planet. The people traveling in it were lucky that most injuries were minor. This patient, though, appeared to have sustained the worst ones. Some appeared not to have been caused by the crash. The other men looked military. This patient wore completely different clothes but was of the same tall stature.

"Well, that was interesting. He appears stable at the moment." The doctor sighed as she scanned the monitors.

"What just happened?" she asked. The others in the room looked as perplexed as she was. "Okay, then let's double check everything. The patient looks humanoid, but obviously his ability to heal is either a natural adaptation or it's been modified. Collect all your data, and let's meet in my office in twenty minutes. And Phillip, see what information you can find on similar physiologies."

The medical team eyed the patient as they wheeled him through the door. Most prisoners were in wards, so she assumed this was someone important. Nothing concerning this man seemed normal, including the two men waiting in the hall.

Doctor Alexis Michaels mentally squared her shoulders as the two men approached her.

"Warden Skinner," she said, as she inclined her head toward the gray-haired man on her right. Turning to the other man, she noted the look of open menace. His left arm was in a fresh cast, and he did not try to hide his impatience.

"Will the prisoner live? Can we move him?" he spat. "This delay is intolerable."

Prisoner? Dr. Michaels thought. *That certainly explains the difference in clothing.*

"Yes, I believe he will recover, but I need to know what I'm dealing with first. Everything went well, but I have a few hundred questions. First, you say he's a prisoner?"

"Before we get into your questions, Doctor, I demand that you keep him sedated. I need to transport him as soon as possible." The man sniffed and turned away from her, as if her demands didn't need to be discussed.

She immediately bristled at his curt tone of dismissal. She was used to dealing with difficult and dangerous people, and this man seemed to be both. She needed him to answer a few questions.

"Who is he, and who the hell are you?" she asked icily.

The calm blue walls of the corridor contrasted with her fiery red hair and hot temper. Her five-and-a-half-feet of bristling energy made her seem like an angry terrier to the prefect. He couldn't find a more fitting comparison. His lip curled as he turned back to face her.

"Who he is, Doctor, doesn't matter. You only need to know he is a criminal I am responsible for, and I wish to transport him as promptly as possible. I am Prefect Tamias of the planet Tyrea."

"In the operating room, something happened I've not encountered before, and I need some answers before proceeding. If I do the wrong thing, I could kill him. For starters, what is his name? We can't call him 'hey you.' And what is he? Is he Tyrean, like yourself? What planet is he from so we can treat him properly. Also, do you have any documentation about his physiology so we can manage his care?"

"Actually, you can call him 'J.' That would be perfect. There will be no more information." The prefect snarled his answer to the doctor. *Yes,* he thought, *call him J on this planet. Just hide him in plain sight. That should work perfectly.*

Dr. Michaels stepped forward to continue her argument, but the warden stepped between them and asked the doctor what had happened in the ER. She pulled her anger back with visible effort.

"I have a meeting in my office in about fifteen minutes to review the feed. Warden, you and the prefect are welcome to attend."

Every operating room had a recorded feed monitoring the actions of prisoners and medical personnel for security. This was SOP (standard operating procedure) at all prisons. She hoped the feed would give them some answers.

"He went from zero vital signs to stable almost before my team could go into action. He isn't human or any other species I know. I need information. His other injuries appear to be older, not life-threatening, and he has a scab-like substance that formed over his worst injuries."

The prefect inhaled sharply. It surprised both her and Warden Skinner when the prefect turned pale.

"Prefect, what's wrong? Do you know what it means?" the warden asked.

He recovered his composure and told them. "He has defenses of his own to help him heal. Again, Doctor, I demand you keep him sedated. He is very dangerous." He turned to the warden. "I expect him to be guarded at all times. Put him in isolation, and keep his room locked."

"Surely these precautions aren't necessary. This is a prison hospital. We already have strict security measures. Medical personnel need to get to patients rapidly. I will not authorize locking the door. That's entirely unnecessary."

"I insist." The prefect turned his back on both of them and walked away.

The warden looked after him and shook his head.

"Carry on, but do NOT lock his door." He nodded to Dr. Michaels and turned back toward his office.

She headed toward her office. She needed a few minutes to recharge after being on her feet for twenty hours straight. She sighed as she sat. The last few days had been brutal at the hospital.

I need a few hours of sleep, she thought. *What I will get is another cup of what the prison calls coffee.*

As she moved around her office, she stretched her five-foot, six-inch frame to loosen tight muscles and fatigue. A framed picture on her wall caught her eye as she paced by it. It made her smile as she remembered it being taken while at college. A group of friends had gotten together to blow off tension and went to a nearby quarry to do some scuba diving. Dan Michaels had been especially touching as he shyly made moves on her. She had really liked Dan, with his steady personality and ready intelligence. He was fun and always friendly with everyone, so it surprised her when he asked her to take a walk in the small wood around the quarry. The more she learned about him, the more she grew to love him. He was so tender after their marriage when they returned to the quarry and made love under the trees. The memory made her shake her head at the bitter-sweet emotions it stirred up. This planet offered placements for both of them. Dan died two years later in a terrible accident. Now she had only memories of a wonderful man. She didn't know why, but the new prisoner reminded her of Dan.

A few minutes later, the medical team assembled in Dr. Michaels' conference room to compare notes. The medical team talked as she sat down at the head of the table. They quieted as they waited for the woman they admired, not only for her skill but also for her willingness to support staff and patients.

"Okay, let's get started. According to all the scanner records and the feed, everything was proceeding normally until he suddenly flat-lined. Let's look at what happened next. I recall Stephen saying we had lost his pulse."

One of the team reached for the paper EKG record, marking a place on it. "Here it is. You can see his heart just stopped."

"What does the EEG say? Does his brain wave scan show anything? A loss of activity, or maybe some bleeding into the subarachnoid space causing brain damage?"

Another team member reached for the EEG sheets. His eyes widened. "I don't think I've ever seen activity like this." He passed the EEG to the person next to him. The readout made the rounds of the team, ending with Dr. Michaels. "Instead of showing some kind of brain damage, it showed extraordinary brain activity. This is *not* the EEG of a patient in a coma, or slipping into a coma, or dying. It might mean an extraordinary ability to repair or separate damaged areas in the brain. One more mystery to add to all the others regarding this patient," the team member added.

"When the substance formed over his injuries, the readings just stopped," Stephen said. "We can extrapolate he suffered from head trauma, heart damage, and maybe other organs, too."

The team studied the readout. Dr. Michaels studied the blood test results that appeared on her computer. She needed more information on Tyrea to compare with what she was seeing.

"Phillip, did you find out anything about Tyrean or any similar physiology?"

Phillip activated the viewing screen to show a minor planet.

"Very little, I'm afraid. Human is the closest physiology. No Tyrean has ever been here. The IntergalNet also had little. The population on Tyrea comes from Terran stock, and they share the same blood types and basic physiology, including atmospheric pressures and structure, but there are some minor differences that come from the differences in planet gravity and nighttime neural patterns because of the longer day and night cycle. Planet gravity is at 0.8, which is less than Earth's 1.0. It would account for his unusual height. It was a long time before trade started on that isolated world. Tyrea is a Class M planet with Earth-like features and atmosphere. It has two polar regions and similar zones as Earth-temperate, tropical, and so on."

The overhead indicator flickered on, interrupting Phillip, and signaled the feed from the ER was ready. Phillip leaned forward and pushed the play button when Dr. Michael nodded okay. It started with the patient being wheeled into the room. He lay completely quiet even though lines of pain were seen on his face and his hands had clenched into fists.

He appears completely human. An unusual looking human, but human, thought Dr. Michaels.

His clothes were constructed of high-quality materials and seemed to be an outdoor outfit. The feed continued showing the team as they studied the various tears in his clothing. After removing them, they studied the various injuries. Some were older, while some looked serious and new. The promptly assessed injuries caused the team to jump into action in what looked like organized chaos. The feed showed the patient to have dyed eyelids of a light blue, and his long hair was a light brown. He was a very tall individual—at least seven feet six inches. An X-ray scan done automatically by the emergency room bed showed his internal organs were basically the same as human, but the arrangement was different, and there seemed to be an extra, unidentifiable organ. It showed the injured organs surrounded by a milky white substance, similar to what had formed around his body. A small disk appeared in his left shoulder.

"Have the tech enlarge this one, ASAP," Dr. Michaels said, then turned to the blood tests, where she found several other anomalies. He had Type-A blood, but the red blood cells seemed extra-large.

"Since we don't know if that's normal, we can only look at these from the closest human baseline. The prefect has clarified that he won't release basic medical records for this patient, so let's keep very careful records of anything else unusual about him. Also, he's a prisoner of Prefect Tamias, who claims he's very dangerous and wants guards stationed outside his room."

"I wouldn't choose to be a prisoner of that man," said Phillip.

"As I was saying, be on guard around him; we don't know what he's capable of doing. Okay, let's keep studying these readouts, and don't be afraid to ask questions. I don't think he can get off the bed, but as ordered by the prefect, guards will be outside the door."

Dr. Michaels knew human stock had moved out into the universe thousands of years ago and settled onto very diverse planets. Insufficient time had elapsed to separate humans into different species, but the different planets had put their own special stamp on each segment. The team settled down to study the differences that Tyrea had stamped on their patient until the next emergency occurred.

CHAPTER 2

Matt O'Shea, head of the Intergalactic Police Force Training Facility, and Lu-zan Cinh, as its head training instructor, made a formidable team. Matt was tall, with the muscular build of a wrestler. He was also innovative, intelligent, and appreciated those qualities in others. Lu-zan was shorter and lightning fast. Both had been impressed by Jon when he applied for the Assistant Survival Specialist position.

Lu-zan was impressed by Jon's knowledge of other worlds and customs. He remembered well the initial interview.

"Why do you want this job?" Lu-zan asked.

"I come from a peaceful planet called Tyrea and have always been fascinated by what my ancestors did to make it peaceful. Planets have different customs and ways to deal with physical and mental stresses in their cultures. These include ritualized movements or meditation techniques that are forms of survival methods, including ritual combat. Knowledge is one of the prime ways to survive in the chaotic universe," he answered.

"Your resume says you have traveled to twenty other planets after graduating from college. Why?"

"We have a long lifespan on my planet, and I probably will not inherit the family business for a very long time. So, I decided to know as much as possible about the universe. Tyrea has only been open to outside trade for a short time, and there is so much to learn."

"But why apply for this position? It's for an expert on teaching survival techniques."

"Several of the planets I visited had areas that called for training in those techniques. I found I had an affinity for that field of study and so took courses to broaden my knowledge. The range of knowledge I gained, I think, can now be applied in the offered position."

Lu-zan was fascinated by this young man, and he felt that this was someone he could teach. After forty years on the job, Lu-zan wanted to retire and pursue his other passion. He knew a lot of the known martial arts and was trying to catalog the unrecorded ones in existence on other known worlds. He was teaching Jon Tor some Tae Kwon Do and Judo moves when Jon Tor went on this last mission. The ancient martial arts from Earth were novelties to Jon. The planet Earth was an unknown planet to Jon, who had not traveled quite so far from his own home planet of Tyrea. The moves fascinated him, and he felt they helped with his coordination, but he also hoped he would never need to use them.

Both valued their friendship highly. He had put more responsibility on the young man's shoulders. As they shared information on their backgrounds, Lu-zan came to realize that Jon would probably have a different destiny awaiting him, but he saw great potential in him. He silently wondered whether he had pushed him too hard or too fast. Now both were faced with a grim reality.

Matt paced in front of Lu-zan, waiting for word to come from the planet Sirius. Sirius was a nasty little Class Q planet on the fringe of the Norris system, with many potential problem spots, like volcanoes and flood zones. It had an unusual orbit around its star that caused the environment to change dramatically throughout the year. The planet also boasted numerous very aggressive predators. It was perfect for training survival specialists. *What could have taken the entire group of trainees so quickly?* wondered Matt. The emergency signal had activated, and no one had responded to repeated attempts to contact them.

Static filled the air. They turned back to the screen that displayed the video feed. The sight that greeted them was grim. The base camp was in shambles, with bodies everywhere. Lieutenant Levison's voice came on as he read a list of the dead.

"Morris, T-Sun, Quinn, Scheck, and Geburson are all dead, sir. Captain Merritt's in critical condition, and there's no sign of Jon Tor anywhere. We're getting ready to scan the surrounding area with heat tracers. S-24 is hovering and awaiting word to begin."

"Carry on, Lieutenant," Matt murmured.

Other screens showed the status of hundreds of other worlds the Intergalactic Police monitored. The training facility had training units on several worlds, but the unit Jon had taken out was to an especially lethal location. Everything appeared normal on all screens except the one they watched.

Matt remembered the last night he saw Jon and the others.

Jon had just finished his presentation to his newest class for camping and survival training—the newest recruits to be agents of the Intergalactic Police Academy. The presentation was before he was to take the group of recent graduates to the planet Sirius. They came from large cities and had the book knowledge, but they had never experienced using survival techniques in a real-world situation.

"Jon, great presentation! Wish I was going with you," Matt said, as he shook the slender man's hand. Turning to the older man who stood next to Jon, he continued. "Are you going with him on this trip, Lu-zan?"

The three men made a sui generis group that couldn't appear more different. Matt, with his wrestler build; Jon, with his height and broad shoulders; and Lu-zan, a man who carried almost an aura of pent-up energy. All looked different, but all had an air of lethal ability.

Lu-zan surveyed the group of men and women from all over the galaxy as they gathered their notes and slowly exited the room. "I'm resting my bones this trip. I'll let Jon do all the hard work."

Jon looked with affection at Lu-zan, who barely came to his shoulders. He knew Lu-zan wanted him to handle the basic camping and survival training in the field. Jon had been with Lu-zan for seven years now. There was genuine affection and respect for one another, and Jon felt Lu-zan was like a second father to him. He missed him dearly, since he couldn't travel to visit as often as he would like. Lu-zan loved Jon like a son, with a bond of trust that had grown between the two men. Lu-zan was the only other person who knew Jon's past.

"Wish I could go, but something came up, and I'm stuck here," said Matt. With its subtle shading in gray, the classroom seemed to reflect the somber mood of the group. Looking at Lu-zan and Jon together always made Matt smile. Lu-zan had to look up to talk to Jon, who bent almost in half to listen.

Re-focusing on the screen, Matt wondered where Jon was in the chaos on the field. Silently, he and Lu-zan watched as the S-24 scanner viewed the area for signs of who had survived or died in the carnage. Image residue would tell them some of the story. Matt grieved for the loss of life and hoped they could help in time to save the injured. The S-24 unit could detect heat signatures for eight hours, so they could study to find out what caused the injuries and death. One member of the group had triggered the SOS beacon so that help could arrive relatively soon, considering the remoteness of the planet. Rescue arrived within four hours, unheard of in the vastness of space, but still not quick enough to save most of the group.

"Sir, the scan shows no one else in the immediate area, but Jon's supplies and gear are here. We found all other members except for two from the planet Borraris. Their supplies and gear are missing."

Another figure tentatively approached the screen and stood at attention, waiting to be acknowledged by the commanding officer. "Sir, I am Private First-Class Para from the planet Born."

"Yes, PFC Para, do you have something to add?" asked Matt.

"Sir, we do a lot of tracking back home. A craft landed over there, and a fight took place there," she said, pointing to the rise behind her. "Someone fell down that rise and probably sustained terrible injuries or death because of the large rocks at the base, but none of these men," she pointed to the bodies being laid out behind them, "have injuries consistent with that type of fall."

"So, what you're saying is one of the missing persons is likely to be severely hurt from a fall down onto those rocks," Matt clarified.

"Yes, sir. We found blood on the rocks and have sent a sample for DNA identification. We should have the results soon."

"Thank you, Private. That information is very helpful."

Lu-zan wandered over to another part of the room where a list of all agents in the field showed on-screen. He also made a copy of a news article. This he pocketed before returning to Matt's side.

"Send me any reports ASAP and include the S-24 scan when it's ready. Make sure you miss nothing." Matt stood with his head bowed.

"Find anything?" Matt asked Lu-zan.

"Can we speak privately, Matt?"

"Of course." Matt led the way to his office, then closed the door and turned.

"Did Jon ever tell you about his family?" Lu-zan asked.

"Just that he was the oldest child of four children, both parents are living, he's from the planet Tyrea, and he doesn't get back to visit often enough."

"Jon may be in big trouble if something about this attack is related to this at all," Lu-zan said, as he handed Matt the printout he had just copied.

"I don't understand. What does the disappearance of Tyrea's ruling party have to do with Jon? Unless there is a coup going on. Where does Jon fit into all this?"

"Let me tell you about Jon."

Two hours later, Matt, Lu-zan, and their team viewed the data from the crash site. From its polished, stainless-steel walls, the room reflected the grim faces of the team as they tried to understand the magnitude of what had happened. Ordinarily, the regular police on a planet would handle the problem, but since it involved a team from the training facility, the police were letting Matt's group handle it. No inter-department rivalry here. This was an attack specifically on their team.

"You already have the infrared scan results showing nothing new. The report by Sergeant Peterson shows an analysis of the wounds inflicted on the dead where they used a cellular disruptor at close range. Logged as missing are Privates Itegia and Morate, both from planet Borraria, and Specialist Jon Tor, from planet Tyrea."

"Thank you," said Matt, and turned to another member of his team with raised eyebrows. The nervous doctor adjusted his tie and picked up his notes. He hated to be the bearer of bad news. He knew they regarded him as the best in his field, but he was in awe of Matt. The man was a legend.

Matt watched him silently, noting that the doctor wouldn't meet his eyes. Matt's anger and frustration level went up another notch. He tried not to direct any of what he felt toward the doctor. He wished he would just make his report.

Finally, the good doctor drew a deep breath and plunged into his report.

"We've completed the brain scan of the officer in charge of the training. He is still critical, so we did a surface scan of his memories. We felt that a deep scan would be too traumatizing. The cellular disrupter hit him on the shoulder, and he subsequently lost the arm and a lot of shoulder muscle. We have started reconstruction measures for the implant of a bio-replacement. We targeted his memory scan to the hour before the deaths. Here's the rest of the relevant information."

He hit a switch on the console in front of him. Overhead, a soundless hologram played, showing the officer scanning the planetary inputs on the shuttle's monitor screen. His hand reached forward and adjusted the feed to the engines as the shuttle slowed, then settled down for the landing. Jon's smiling face came into view, followed by the rest of the party. His view changed as he looked at the angry planet through the shuttle window. The sky showed an ugly yellow tint from the volcanic ash pumping into the atmosphere and descending on the distant jagged terrain. He got out of the captain's chair and turned to check his crew member's facemask. He then led the crew out of the shuttle and surveyed the landing site.

Here, the doctor stopped the recording. "The initial survey had picked this landing site because of its relative stability." Again, he restarted the recording.

Men and women swiftly set up their tents and organized the camp. They kept guns ready in case one of the powerful predators came to investigate the activity. The recording showed a wet, gray day made sludgy by the ash, and showed the team slipping on rocks and grass as they moved around. Jon gestured to the bucket and water sterilizer he held as if he were going for water, and he disappeared from sight. The captain helped with the organization of the camp and seemed to move toward a ridge showing his hands handling various rocks, while a catalog of shapes and types were displayed inside his mask with an analysis of temperature range. This confirmed his faith that the camp site was stable. Gradually, he moved farther and farther away from the camp.

"That goes on for another 34.3 minutes," Dr. Tononia informed them. "With your permission, we'll jump to the part where he comes back."

The view differed from the other side as he slowly scanned the camp, showing most of the tents erected, the campfire burning with a pan tilted, its contents burning and giving off a lot of smoke. Everything seemed eerily quiet, with bodies lying at all angles and positions, men and women caught unawares by cellular disrupter fire from people they trusted. His view showed one of the two agents from Borraria turn his way, and the view moved hastily as the captain took cover. The view inched around rocks and bushes until it showed another view of the camp. It moved toward the largest tent. A hand appeared with a large knife, and he slipped into the interior. The view panned the space and showed no one in the tent. His focus moved to the transmitter and pushed the emergency locator button. The slightest noise would alert the terrorists to his presence. He jammed the switch on, and the reassuring light came on. He immediately kicked the transmitter to the other part of the tent. His actions saved him and allowed a full ten second burst to be broadcast before a second beam destroyed the machine. A third beam hit him. He was still conscious as he saw Jon appear, still carrying the water bucket he had gone to fill. Jon's face reflected his racing emotions for all to see. Astonishment, concern, puzzlement, and lastly rage all raced across his face as he realized what had happened. He dropped the bucket.

"Why?" he seemed to say, as he defiantly faced the armed terrorists.

One tech watching in the room began to lip read as the action unfolded on-screen.

The view changed as the officer turned his head.

"They need you at home, Your Highness. I suggest you submit peacefully."

The officer saw Jon suddenly twist and try to roll, but he slipped on the grass and a disrupter beam hit as he tumbled over the ledge. The greenery blocked his line of vision, so he turned his head to see the terrorists.

"Quick, make sure he's still alive, you idiot," one terrorist shouted, as he gestured with his gun.

Periods of blank screen interrupted scenes of Jon being dragged back to the top of the ledge and loaded onto a transport board. The last view was of a small, short-range cargo carrier landing a short distance away. Finally, the recording stopped.

Matt sat, not believing what he'd just seen, staring at the blank screen. *Jon, what have they done to you?*

"We need to look at what's happening on Tyrea."

CHAPTER 3

Dr. Michaels slowly explored the largest injury, looking for some hint of what the white substance was that covered the area, but it was seamless, with a semi-soft covering that felt soft but wouldn't let her palpate the wound. She tried for a strand or two for analysis, but that didn't work. Then she tried to cut a sample using a surgical knife, but again was unsuccessful. She smiled ruefully at the knife. Maybe a laser would work. All the other injuries showed a healthy color with no unusual swelling or redness. His present condition bordered on the miraculous. The patient's breathing was unlabored and deep as in sleep, not a coma, as his brain scans seemed to show.

"Dr. Michaels, here is the prelim criminal scan on this patient. I thought you should see it." The nurse handed her a small, clear plexitext sheet.

"A criminal scan?"

"Nobody told me not to do one. You know its standard procedure."

"My fault, I apologize. I forgot to relay the new orders of the prefect for this particular patient. I'm sorry."

"I just don't want trouble for following standard procedure."

Dr. Michaels gave her a slight smile. "I know. It will be all right, I promise."

The nurse sniffed and walked away.

Dr. Michaels decided she would have to get over her snit on her own. There wasn't much she could do about it, but she hoped it didn't blow up in their faces. Then she realized she could learn more about her fascinating patient by reading what was in her palm.

"What will be all right, Doctor?" The gruff voice of the warden sounded from the nearby doorway. She shoved the scan into the second chart of the four she had in her hands, then turned to face him.

"I told her it would be all right to take some time off," she lied.

The nurse looked back at the warden and nodded her agreement. Warden Skinner waved impatiently. "Sure, sure. How long do you need? You can take a little time off."

"Oh, just an hour or two. Sir, if that's okay?"

"Fine, then see you later." He moved to let her through the doorway. Turning back to Dr. Michaels, he narrowed his eyes.

"Dr. Michaels, I was in the John Doe's room earlier and according to the readings on him, he's not in an induced coma as ordered, but in a deep, normal sleep. Would you care to explain?"

She pulled her shoulders back, tried to look taller, and reminded herself that she was a professional and a physician and the warden was neither. A sense of calm came over her.

"As you know, this patient sustained severe trauma of the chest cavity, ribcage, and femur in his right leg. We're still not sure if there is brain damage. We need a neural brain scan, and I would prefer he be aware so we can better evaluate him. Plus, the blood tests have come back. His blood is Type-A but has a lot of unknown elements in it, and we don't have enough information in our database to identify them. We are dealing with a lot of uncertainties here."

"The prefect does not want him awake. He has his reasons, even though he has not seen fit to share them with me." Warden Skinner sniffed with a scowl on his face. He did not like being told what to do to run his prison.

"The prefect is not a doctor. He also demands we save this patient and then ties our hands," she replied hotly.

"Okay, Doctor." He motioned with his hands, pacifying her. "I'll allow the patient to be brought to consciousness for those tests. Then sedate him again. Do everything quietly, Doctor. Do we understand one another?"

Dr. Michaels gave him a quick nod and a little smile before she turned and hurried down the hall. After she finished rounds, she called her team together and outlined the plan and the need for secrecy. No one on her team would betray them; the prefect had made no friends with his high-handed demands. Even his soldiers rolled their eyes behind his back, but they jumped to do his bidding. Her team would do their best to keep out of his way.

As they filed out to begin "Operation Wooly Eyes," she pulled the crim-scan out. Standard procedure where a patient has no identification was to take fingerprints, a DNA scan, and a retinal scan. These were fed into the prison computer for a match, and if it made no match, the computer automatically requested a match from the databank at the Interplanetary Police complex.

Absently she toed her shoes off under her desk. After being on her feet for so long, it felt like heaven. *The problem is I'll have to put them on again, which is going to hurt worse,* she thought.

"Hmm, surprise, surprise, no match on prison records, but what have we here?" she murmured. There was a notation from the databank at Intergalactic Police Academy. "Request noted, security clearance requested. Please contact 3-001-231-0004-IPA immediately." She picked up the phone, dialed the number, and wondered whether she was digging her own grave. The warden, she knew, would take a very dim view of this.

She heard a powerful male voice come over the phone. "Matt O'Shea, how can I help you? And how did you get this number?"

"This is Dr. Michaels of the Greenwich Prison Facility. We sent a routine inquiry to the IPA regarding an injured prisoner at our facility, and I received a request for us to contact this number."

"What's the name of your prisoner, Dr. Michaels?"

"We don't have a name, Mr. O'Shea. He is a survivor of a crash on our planet and was brought here to the prison medical center for treatment. He is here with the Prefect Tamias from the planet Tyrea. The prefect says he is a dangerous prisoner being taken back to Tyrea."

"Dr. Michaels," Matt responded excitedly, "I have your request on my computer now. The man you say is a dangerous prisoner is actually one of our survival instructors. They abducted him from a base camp yesterday. What is his condition? Have you talked with him at all?"

Dr. Michaels heard a shoe scuff outside her door, and then the door began to open. She talked alertly and in a slightly louder voice into the mouthpiece. "Of course, Doctor, I'll look in on your patient first thing tomorrow morning if that's soon enough."

"Did someone come in and you can't talk?"

"Yes, that's right."

"Okay, stall for time. We have a situation that seems to be related, so I or my representative will come ASAP. One of us should be there in about ten hours. I'll keep you informed as to who is coming." He disconnected the link.

"Fine, I'm glad to help and have a great vacation," she said into the dead phone. The fine hairs on her neck rose as she looked up to see the prefect standing in the office doorway.

"Yes, Prefect, how can I help you?"

"I came to tell you I want the prisoner readied to be moved by tomorrow afternoon. There is a ship available, and I mean to take it."

"Your prisoner is in no condition to travel anywhere. Tomorrow is too soon."

"You must get him ready. This delay is intolerable."

"And if he doesn't survive the trip?"

"Oh, he will survive. Tyrea will not let him die now."

"What do you mean, 'Tyrea will not let him die now?' And I still have tests to run and medical questions that need answers."

"That doesn't matter. He needs to travel to Tyrea as promptly as possible. See to it at once."

"Why the hurry?" But he dismissed her and her question as he walked out of her office.

This gets curiouser and curiouser, she thought. *Who is Matt O'Shea that he or whomever he sends will jump on a ship and travel to the prison for this patient?*

She did a database check on his name that had her eyebrows climbing. Matt O'Shea was the director of the entire Intergalactic Police Academy.

Why would a prisoner's phone number or whatever he is go directly to the director of IPA? She decided it was a past time she checked on her mysterious patient. *Still no name,* she thought. *There are definitely conflicting stories between the prefect and this Matt O'Shea. If he is correct, then the prefect is guilty of very serious criminal behavior.*

Dr. Michaels hurried to her patient's room. The cube of a room with its pale blue walls, painted to be restful, seemed bigger since the only furniture was the bed with its built-in monitor, a small cabinet that held medical supplies, and a chair to help relieve its starkness. There she found him blinking at her assistant, Stephen, as he tried to communicate with the patient. She saw the wary look and concluded that he probably understood what was being said.

"Hello there," she said cheerfully, as she moved to the side of the bed. "We haven't met yet, but I'm your doctor while you are in this hospital. My name is Dr. Michaels, and you are at the Greenwich Prison Medical Facility. This is my assistant, Stephen." She took in the puzzled look on his face. "You were in a crash, and the Prefect of Tyrea transported you here for treatment." She observed him for his reaction. It did not disappoint her, as he tried to get out of the bed.

The medical assistant gently pushed him back. "He seems to understand me, but I haven't heard him say a word." He turned back to the bed. "That's okay," he said, patting the patient's arm. "We'll talk later."

"I'll talk to him a little now." Looking at her assistant, she said, "Please keep watch for the prefect or warden, will you? Warn us if either comes this way."

He smiled at both of them. "Operation Woolly Eyes is under way."

Turning back to the patient, she needed to address his most pressing issues first.

"Okay, let me start. You have serious injuries impossible to treat because a substance has formed over them. The substance seems to be normal for you, and I don't know enough about Tyrean physiology to be able to deal with it. Also, I sent your fingerprints, retina scan, etc. to the IPA for ID, over I might add, the prefect's and the warden's objections or knowledge. I talked with a Mr. Matt O'Shea at the IPA, and he or whomever he sends is on their way here and should arrive in about ten hours." She noticed the way he immediately relaxed at the mention of O'Shea's name. Okay, so that must mean he knows who O'Shea said he was.

A whisper of a sigh and a soft murmur of "Matt's coming." He closed his eyes; she noticed his eyes in the emergency room because they were an unusual color of silver.

"I take it you know this Matt O'Shea?"

"Yes." He whispered a breathy, "Thank you."

"Don't thank me yet. We have a problem. The prefect wants to leave with you by tomorrow afternoon."

"Then I must leave now." He tried to turn to his side and noticed the restraints.

"What the…? Why am I restrained? Please, I must go!" He started jerking on them so hard he shook the bed.

"Wait, don't pull on those. You will hurt yourself more. We will figure something out." She tried to hold his hands still and calm him as he continued to struggle against the bonds.

"Take them off, take them off now. Please." He pleaded as he struggled. "Why won't you help me? If you're helping me, then take them off. You don't even know me. Please take them off."

"I can't take them off right now, but I promise you I will return soon. And you're right, I don't know you. I don't even know your real name." Walking to the window, she told him bluntly, "I talked with your Matt O'Shea. He's the head of the Intergalactic Police Academy, and he told me you're not a prisoner at all. The prefect is claiming you are a dangerous criminal. Why is the prefect doing this to you?" She walked back to the bed. "You know, working here, you see all kinds of criminals. Some are dangerous, desperate, or innocent, but in reality, most are guilty. I feel your prefect should be in that bed, not you. Something is not right, and this hospital is being used. I dislike being used. Can you tell me why I'm being used?"

"I must go to Tyrea. I must get to my home world. Something terrible must have happened."

Alexis weighed what he said and shrugged. Even though he wouldn't trust her, she still had a choice: help him or let the prefect take him tomorrow. She couldn't let the prefect have his way. She just didn't trust him. She hoped it was the right thing to do. All she had to go on was her gut feeling.

"All right then. Rest. That's doctor's orders. The prefect ordered you restrained and sedated. I will not sedate you, so be quiet and keep your eyes shut at all times. My staff or I will let you know when you can open your eyes or speak. Rest." She gave his hand a squeeze to encourage him.

"My name is…"

She stopped him.

"No, don't tell me or any of my staff. We might accidentally say it at the wrong time or to the wrong person. I trust my team, but not so much some others. It would be a disaster if someone accidentally said it to the wrong person."

Wearily he nodded agreement and closed his eyes. Soon he slept, so fast she wondered whether he was still in pain, but he had been in rugged outdoor clothing. Maybe he had mastered the art of sleeping anywhere, like soldiers did.

Dr. Michaels hurried to her office and paged her team. After they had arrived in her conference room, she told them of what she had found on the crim-scan and of her conversation with Matt O'Shea. The reaction to that was very positive, and encouraged by what she proposed next, she outlined her plan. Timing was very important if they were to get him away tonight. All of them agreed to help. She wanted them to be protected from any repercussions. She didn't know how much power the prefect had. He sometimes seemed harsh, but he seemed fair—at times very demanding in his dealings with prisoners and staff. The soldiers that the prefect had with him concerned her the most. They were meanspirited except around the prefect. They seemed very afraid of him.

She asked herself, *Is the prefect putting on an act?*

"Should we get down to some planning?" And so, they did.

"Thanks, everyone, for your support." She tried to convey her appreciation as they left the room. They each squeezed her arm and gave her a brief smile as most of them filed out.

CHAPTER 4

Matt warily told the team to go home and pack. "Get a good night's sleep. It will be a long trip to Sirius." He turned to Lu-zan, preparing to leave. "Lu-zan, I wish I could travel with you, but I need to oversee this mess on Sirius."

"No, Matt, say hello to Desiree for me. I'll take care of it and will keep you informed."

Matt hurried home to see Desiree and to pack. He hated leaving his family on these trips, but emergencies happened, and this time it had happened to his team and Jon, who was a friend. There was no question he would help.

"Going on vacation or are you leaving me?" she asked. Smiling, she moved into the room. "What's going on?" She gave him a hug and a hearty kiss, then stepped back. "Now, tell me."

"I wish I could tell you more, but Jon is in the middle of it. Lu-zan is leaving to deal with the fact that Jon has been taken from the attack site—by whom, we don't know yet. I'm going to Sirius to deal with the attack site."

"I hate it when you get called away. And this sounds serious. Jon is already hurt, but Lu-zan or you could also get hurt!" she said. "I'd better get this packing done before the kids get done with their homework. When do you leave?"

"Not till early morning. We have time for a proper goodbye." He kissed her, took the shirt she was mangling out of her hands, and slowly backed her against the bed. Slowly, he showed her how much he would miss her. Later, they had a quiet dinner and extra family time with the children. When the morning came, he would leave, but his family would know he loved and cherished them.

Meanwhile, Lu-zan had flown to the island he called home and retreated into the room he referred to as his inner sanctum. He had a brief span of time till his ship arrived for the trip to Greenwich, so he would think on the matter while he waited. It was his most private room, his meditation room. He and his wife had lovingly decorated it in the ancient way of their ancestors, and it reflected their eclectic tastes. The serene feeling he always felt when sitting by his simplistic garden just wouldn't materialize. The gentle silver of the foliage reminded him of Jon's eyes, and his own eyes kept misting till he could no longer see the combed sand. He looked over at the hologram of his late wife on the bamboo wall bordering the garden. He had placed it there so he could consult her when troubled and needed her guidance. They had not been blessed with children. Then Jon had come into his world. He wished Bahia could have known him, but she was long dead. Oh, how he missed her gentle smile and wise counsel.

He quietly lowered the lights and took his lotus position on the mat. There, he prayed and meditated on Jon's life. Lu-zan had shared his home, his planet, and his knowledge with Jon. Jon had shared stories of his family, the history of his planet, and his ambitions for his world and people. Jon had become like a son to him, but Lu-zan did not believe in coincidence. He believed Jon had entered his life for a purpose. He felt this was the reason now.

His ship would arrive in a few minutes, so he got up to grab his pack.

CHAPTER 5

Lu-zan had slept and now sat staring out of the porthole that showed the silvery stream of space as it bent around the ship. He wished someone had invented a faster mode of travel than hyperspace travel. Eight hours ago, he had learned of Jon's danger, and now he was hurtling through space trying to save his friend. Lu-zan had spent hours combing through records from Tyrea, looking for any information on its ruling family. When he'd first met Jon, he had also studied its political system, which until recently had been very stable, if unusual.

He thought about the political makeup of Tyrea. They had a ruling family, and a Congress of Senators made up of each of the three Providences. There was only one government on the entire planet. The ruling royal family was to maintain the energy from the planet's core. Lu-zan didn't know how it worked. Jon had simply told him they keep power flowing in a balanced manner. The planet had been politically stable for over 1,000 years, but only about one hundred and fifty years ago had it been opened to galactic trade.

He was getting a headache from staring at monitors for hours. He had two choices: he could wait for news or take a nap. Taking a coin from his pocket, he flipped it. The nap won, so he closed his eyes.

Later, he reviewed what information he had so far. The trouble on Tyrea was not a simple government takeover. Information coming out of Tyrea was not reliable. General Tariq, the acting military governor, was claiming outside agents were responsible. The planet itself was in turmoil, and a general feeling of panic was brewing. A two-pronged hunt had started for the first-born son of King Borig-Tor. General Tariq was conducting one hunt, and the other was an unofficial hunt by members of the populace. The first son's name was Jon-Tor—his Jon. IPA agents on Tyrea said the populace seemed to believe Jon would save them. Lu-zan wondered whether the populace wanted Jon to save them from General Tariq or from a planet gone wild—or both. Ancient mechanical systems were shutting down, and no one could get them stabilized again. The people cried, saying it was the revenge of the Tor family against General Tariq. Rumors abounded that General Tariq had, in fact, murdered the ruling family. Legend older than most of the written records said they directly linked the welfare of the planet to the family of Tor.

Lu-zan's mind swirled with facts, figures, and suppositions on Tyrea. He felt his head would burst with them, then he felt the slight tingle on his wrist. He activated the buzzing wrist communicator. A center section of the band dissolved to show the watch agent in the command center at IPA.

"Sorry to disturb your sleep, sir, but we just received word from Borraria that they found the two agents who were scheduled to go on the survival training. The training mission left port before their bodies were found in their homes by family members. We are continuing to investigate the two imposters on the mission, sir."

"Try to match them with IDs from a crash on the planet Greenwich. Contact me if you find anything." Exhausted, his mind worn thin with worry, finally Lu-zan slipped into an uneasy sleep.

CHAPTER 6

Jon drifted in and out of sleep. Flashes of memory popped into his mind like fireworks. He remembered coming around the bend in the path. The rest was a blur of bodies, the stun, the sudden pain, and the fall off the world. "I can't lose you now," a woman's voice kept repeating in his dreams. He liked the voice and felt protected.

A voice from the foot of his bed almost jolted him into opening his eyes. He hoped the small movement he had made was not noticeable. That voice seemed vaguely familiar, but he couldn't place it. A smell of strong aftershave permeated his senses. Again, he tried to place where he knew the aroma, but he couldn't. At least he had his hearing and sense of smell. He hoped his other senses would come back, too, he thought, as he fought to make sense of everything being said around him.

"How are the preparations going for moving him, Doctor?"

"Prefect, I strongly object to this. Please re-consider this decision. He is too weak to be moved. He needs more time to heal. Is there at least a medic on the ship?"

"Doctor, I'm warning you. He is leaving tomorrow, ready or not. He can get medical attention on Tyrea. I cannot repair my ship on time, and there is a transport ship available. I intend to be on it with my prisoner, with or without your permission. You don't know how to treat him anyway. You said so yourself. I'm doing you a favor by taking him off your hands. We take off tomorrow at 1700 hours your time. I suggest you do your job and prepare him."

"What does the warden say?"

The prefect bristled.

"Why bring the warden into it? He has no say in this. Have him readied by 1500 hours so we can get to the spaceport. Believe me, Doctor, you will regret it if you don't obey my orders. Get it done."

The retreating footsteps and the door closing signaled his withdraw from the room. Jon waited.

"It's okay. Open your eyes now," came the whispered words. "I really don't like that man."

Jon opened his eyes to find Dr. Michaels staring at him.

What does she see? he wondered. *What is she thinking?*

He worried she would decide she did not want to help him. He wouldn't blame her or her staff if they wanted to back out. She seemed to see his fear and uncertainty because she sighed and relaxed.

"You don't have to do this, you know. I wouldn't think less of you and your staff if you didn't help me." He didn't want any of them to suffer because of him. People he valued had already died because of him, and he dreaded the reason for all the death.

She shook her head, as if coming out of a daze.

"Did you recognize him?" she asked.

"I think I know him, but it's hazy," he answered, his forehead furrowed in thought.

"Don't push it, I'm sure it will come to you."

"Please take off the restraints. I need to move my arms and legs, or I won't be able to move later."

"I agree." She removed the restraints and helped him get some feeling back by rubbing his limbs. "Do you want to stand?" she asked, after she checked his injuries.

Slowly, hesitantly, Jon moved his legs over the side of the bed. He put his feet on the floor and slid his weight onto his feet. Swaying, but using the bed as a brace, he found his balance and glanced up to see Dr. Michaels smiling at him.

"Very impressive, considering a few hours ago you couldn't move. Let's try to walk to that chair." She encouraged him by taking his arm.

Jon slowly walked to the chair and, feeling triumphant, he smiled as he sat down. Walking that small distance felt great but wouldn't get him somewhere more secure. He needed more exercise, fast. Getting up, he again walked slowly to the bed and back. The small room was twelve square feet and reflected the security measures needed, like bars at the window, an alarm on the wall, and a security camera. Even the bed was a standard issue with bio readouts. Jon eyed the security camera warily.

"I need to leave tonight."

Dr. Michaels started.

"Okay, we need you to try on these clothes," she said, as she passed him a bundle from the closet and turned away to give him some privacy. "These are courtesy of Phillip. I hope they fit. You are rather tall."

Jon, though surprised and pleased that she seemed to understand his urgency, did not understand her motivation in helping. "Why are you doing this?"

He thought she would not answer his question when she said, "You need to walk a little more to exercise those unused muscles. You're still very faint from your injuries, but it's miraculous how well and fast they have healed. Take the boots and all except underwear off, and we'll put them in the closet till needed and then put your hospital gown on over your clothes. I'm sure either the prefect or one of his soldiers will shortly check on you. I'll be back after I do my rounds and lead you down the stairs."

"I'm sorry your staff might suffer, but I must get out of here. I still don't understand why you and your staff are doing this for me. None of you know me."

"I promise we will discuss that later. Right now, you need to exercise a little."

He meekly put on the hospital gown, and she bundled the boots and other clothes into the closet.

"How do you plan to get me out of here?"

She outlined her plan as he walked back and forth in the small room. He could see how worried she was. She could see he was still dismayed by what she was asking him to do, but he was determined to not let her down, or his family, or his planet. He still didn't understand her motivation for helping him. She had a lot to lose if she did this, but he had to go back to Tyrea.

"Get back in bed," she said apologetically. He stiffened when she picked up the restraints.

"Do you have to put them back on as well?"

"I'm afraid so, just in case."

She made them a little looser. She left him with his restless mind to worry the time away until evening. The barred window shed little light into the room. His eyelids slowly closed as sleep claimed him. He dreamed of freedom and fell into a fitful daze. As the light left the small window, Jon became aware of soft footsteps moving around the bed. He was careful not to show his startlement when a hand touched his wrist and checked the restraints. A breath stirred his hair, and he tried not to tense as a whisper sounded next to his ear. The smell of aftershave again teased his senses, tugging at a memory.

"You are the last, Jon-Tor, and as soon as we have your secrets, you will be no more. You can dream of reaching your family. Within two more nights, you will have told us all we need to know, and then you will beg us to kill you. You can dream of accompanying your family in glorious death, but not yet. Not just yet, Jon-Tor. First, you will give us the secret of TOR." Then the footsteps receded, and Jon was alone.

Jon finally recognized the voice as one he knew well. Prefect Tamias was not there to see the tears track down Jon's face as he grieved for his lost family.

The prefect had said he could join his family, but not yet. Did that mean they were being held somewhere and he would kill them all, or were they already dead and the prefect would kill him, too? His exhausted mind raced with all the possibilities. Jon tried to stay awake, but the little exercise he had gotten earlier, and his uncertain condition, soon had him falling into a nightmare-filled sleep.

CHAPTER 7

Dr. Michaels returned to J's room quietly. One second, he was alone; the next, he was being gently shaken awake, and the doctor was urging him up and helping him to put on his clothing and boots. He was still healing, and he knew he needed the sleep. He became more awake as he put on the boots. Soon, they slipped out of his room silently. The hallways were dimly lit, and they moved cautiously from shadow to shadow. Jon looked back and saw a nurse talking to one of the prefect's men, keeping him from seeing them as they went down the hall. He tried to move quickly, but found he had to make frequent stops to rest. As they moved downward, a trip that should have lasted five minutes seemed to take three times as long, but Dr. Michaels waited patiently for him to get his breath, and quietly urged him to keep moving. In the basement, Phillip met them with harnesses, which he silently put on Jon while Dr. Michaels put hers on as well. Phillip had his own harness handy, but he did not don it. At J's look, Phillip smiled at him and mouthed, "Later."

Turning, Phillip lifted a large metal cover from a raised portion of the floor. He strapped a length of rope to Dr. Michaels' harness and lowered her down into the hole. She descended quickly, and once she was in the underground river, she grabbed one of the iron handles that ran along the passageway. Someone had originally put these handles along the side of the tunnel for the convenience of maintenance men. Now they would use them to help escape the prison.

Dr. Michaels turned to the opening above her to watch for J.

Jon could hear rushing water, though he couldn't see it in the hole's darkness. He closed his eyes and shivered. Phillip gave his shoulder a squeeze of encouragement. Then the rope in Phillip's hand gave a tug, and it was his turn to be lowered. He saw the slick walls of the access tunnel. He could feel the dampness all around him and hear the rushing sound of water. The drop was longer than he expected, but soon even the walls disappeared from sight and touch. All he could hear was the increasing sound of rushing water. After what felt like forever, he felt the icy fingers of the water itself as he lowered into the frigid, underground river.

Jon screamed. Blinding pain seared through him as the freezing water engulfed him. With a flash of white light, Jon felt his body go rigid as a white web enveloped him. He fought for control, but no matter how he struggled against the stiffness of the web, it surrounded and immobilized him. Soon he could see nothing, and his world turned dark. Eventually, even that faded away.

Dr. Michaels whirled around as she heard J cry out. She flinched and watched in horror as she witnessed the unexpected transformation. The cocoon fell and floated free on the river. She just caught a part of J's harness as it floated behind the cocoon that had been J a moment ago. It almost tore through her grip as the river tried to tug the cocoon downstream. She panted from the pull of the current as she tried to control it. It was like trying to control a bucking horse. Finally, she brought it closer and under control in a nearby eddy.

"Well, you are just full of surprises. I wondered how I was going to get you down the river. Please, just don't sink," she told the cocoon. "Here we go."

She put the strap from his harness around her waist and, using the cocoon as a floatation device, they started off down the river.

They were under the prison proper but would run into trouble where the river emerged from under the walls. There was a gate Phillip had to open for them and sensors had to be turned off. Phillip would join them at that point. She would need Phillip's strength to keep them from going over the falls a mile away. They would have about a half mile to get to safety. The river had a strong current that would only move faster as it neared the edge of the falls.

The sound of the moving water changed as the darkness lightened around them. The noise of rushing water no longer reverberated off the walls, and she could see the light brighten. She swam strongly toward the side. The pull of the water was getting stronger, and she was already tiring, as she could feel her arms and legs weakening. The underground bank of the river seemed far away. Too soon, it was right in front of her, and the grate was only ten feet away. They needed to reach the side before the grate went up so she could control the cocoon.

She battled the debris out of the way to grab the handle sticking out from the wall. The grate was just rising out of the water when she struggled to control the cocoon and hold desperately onto the handle. Looking around, she spied a little ledge protruding above the waterline. She pushed the cocoon up onto it and turned to look back.

Phillip doesn't know about the cocoon, she thought. *But he also won't be trusting J to be much help since he was so weak. I hope it's waterproof. J's life depends on it.*

Phillip came into view and grabbed the other handle next to hers.

"What happened?" He eyed the cocoon.

"I'll explain later. Let's get someplace more secure than this. How much time do you think we have before they find the grate open and the sensors off?"

"I figure about an hour. If we're lucky, we'll have until the maintenance man reports for work tomorrow. One nurse volunteered to turn the sensors on if she can get there unnoticed. Are you okay? The current is pretty strong."

"Yes, I think I'll be okay. I just need a minute to rest. Won't there be a sensor light if something large goes out the grate?" This had been a major imperfection point in her plan.

"No alert on this grate," he shouted over the sound of rushing water. "Apparently, no one has tried to escape this way before. I can't imagine why no one has ever tried," he said with a grin.

The chilly water swept her and Phillip out from under the walls of the prison to float out under a cloudless sky.

A beautiful day to go swimming with a cocoon, Alexis thought.

They swam strongly to the right side of the river, towing the cocoon. The river continued to gather strength and speed as it travelled toward the fall over the cliff about a half-mile ahead. They both saw the rope and grabbed for it with one hand. The other hand held the cocoon between them, which bucked and swayed. She looked up to see Sue leaning out over the river, trying to help. The doctor let go of the cocoon and grabbed the offered hand. Sue pulled hard, and Phillip pushed the doctor and the cocoon to solid ground. Alexis finally found her footing and dragged her body up the bank. She pulled on the cocoon, which bobbed and wrestled to get away. Phillip made a last push of it toward her, and it sailed up onto the bank. Sue immediately turned to help Phillip up onto the bank.

"I don't want to do that again, ever," she said, as she wrung out her wet clothes.

"I agree," Phillip said, as he and Sue fought for their breath.

Sue looked over at the cocoon. "I take it that this is our patient. What the hell happened to him?"

"There was a flash of light as soon as he hit the water, and this happened. When he is out of this, he and I are going to have a talk."

"*If* he comes out of this," added Phillip thoughtfully.

"Stay optimistic," Sue remonstrated.

"Help me get him farther up the bank and under some cover. It must be some kind of normal protective reaction, but I certainly have seen nothing like it before. It looks like the same white scab stuff that formed in the ER."

The three of them pushed and pulled the cocoon under the trees. Alexis could see the cave peeking out of the nearby hidden grove of trees.

"I stashed some supplies in the cave like you asked, and if you need help, there is a transmitter tuned to my son's scout troop frequency. Just be careful what you say. We use it all the time to call the kids home. Our family code name is dog star75. I have to get back home, so I'm nice and innocent when the search starts. Good luck."

Phillip coiled the rope and packed up items Sue had handy in case of trouble, and Alexis turned to the cocoon. She could see a trail from the water to the cocoon. Grabbing a tree branch from the ground, she started to erase the tracks. The area, deeply forested with old-growth timber and next to no undergrowth, made is easier to move through, but also easier to track. Silently, they both picked up the cocoon and started moving toward the cave. It took three trips. One to get J there, one for their packs and harnesses, and one to finish wiping the trail clean.

"Let's hope any pursuers don't have heat sensors with them," Phillip said, as he scanned the sky.

"How many employees know about this cave?" Alexis worried the cave was too close to the prison. Surely searchers could spot it. She looked around for bush and fallen limbs to disguise the opening. She spied some larger limbs that might work.

"Most of the families living around here know—maybe not prison employees. I don't think we should stay here for very long anyway. It seems to me it's a little too close to the prison, but we'll get you and our guest out as soon as possible."

"We can use some of those tree limbs."

Phillip nodded his agreement. "That sounds like a good idea."

They carried J into the cave. One of the dark gray walls curved back to the right, making an area out of line of sight. The dry floor was rock strewn and uneven, causing Alexis to trip twice.

"Keep going. It gets better," Phillip informed the doctor.

As they continued to move back farther into the cave, it surprised Alexis to find that it curved around into a larger chamber. The cave blossomed up and glowed with beautiful shades of red and gold. She studied the walls, trying to figure out how they had formed.

"Wow, this is pretty amazing. How far back does it go?" she asked.

"About a hundred yards, with a lot of twists. The ceiling heights also vary. A couple of chambers are a little smaller than this one. Some are really tiny. It is really a whole cave system."

"Maybe we should explore to see if there is a spot we can retreat to if they find this cave."

"We can block a small side spot. It's next to a larger chamber, so maybe we should camp there. I'll look at it after we get J settled somewhere a little safer."

"Good plan. Phillip, please call me Alexis. It seems silly to be so formal, considering the situation. Why do all the staff call me Dr. Michaels anyway?"

"The warden warned everyone to never call you by your first name. No one knew why. We assumed you just didn't like to be called Alexis."

"Maybe we can change that. It's silly. J's friend at IPA is coming here. We can plan to let him know where J is without alerting anyone. You ought to travel back to the prison so they don't suspect you, or go home so you're there when they check on you. You really don't want your wife to meet them alone."

"I don't want to leave you here, but I see your point. But first, let's get you and J settled, and I'll check out that potential hidey-hole."

"Okay, I'll check the supplies Sue brought. Eat first. We can plan better. I'm hungry. I want a look at this cocoon."

They continued moving into the cave until they came to a smaller area several twists away from the opening. There they found the supplies. Alexis noticed a nice ledge projecting from the left side of the cavern. They placed the cocoon on the ledge and pulled the bags of supplies over to that side. She was glad to see that Sue had included sleeping bags, flashlights, and a small stove in the supplies, which included her doctor's bag.

Yippee. We can make real coffee. Not what a lot of people call "coffee." I can survive, she thought.

They made a quick lunch from the supplies and then finished wiping their trail. Phillip was as good as his word and checked for the hidey-hole. Fortunately, it was close, and Alexis could hide J and their supplies there. A rock screen even shielded the opening to the small area. It would be tight, but doable.

Phillip left to go home at dawn the next day. Alexis gave him Matt O'Shea's number so he could contact Matt or whomever he sent when he arrived. Phillip had told her he could call a friend at the spaceport and check the scheduled arrival of the ship.

Alexis moved to check on J. The cocoon seemed seamless. *Maybe like the cocoon of a silkworm,* she thought. *Find the starting point and just unwrap.* So, she ran her hands carefully over the surface. Not finding any convenient or obvious loose thread, she started looking for a crack or line. Again, nothing showed on the surface of the cocoon. She studied the material. It looked like the same substance that had formed over his earlier injuries.

She sat back and sighed. "Come on, J, I need you to come out of this cocoon," she demanded. Under her hands, the cocoon warmed, surprising her so much she jumped. With her heart in her throat, she leaned in and talked to him. "Come on, J, come back to me." The cocoon continued to warm, but nothing else seemed to happen. She continued to talk to him, since there didn't seem to be anything else she could do to speed the process.

She was rubbing her sore throat when the cocoon moved. It didn't rock, but it bulged in places. She noticed that the areas that bulged were over the areas of major injuries on his body.

Maybe the white substance that formed in the emergency room wasn't waterproof, and when J hit the water, his body reacted with a normal reaction to protect, she thought.

Running her hands over the cocoon, she noticed an increase in the activity, so she continued hoping she was helping the healing and not doing harm. She sighed again. She just had no way of knowing.

An hour later, she noticed that the activity was slowing, and the cocoon was turning more transparent.

"Okay, what are my options?" she debated with herself. Should she continue to rub the cocoon or stop? Should she talk to J again? She just didn't know enough, which made her angry. "I'm a doctor! I should know what to do, dammit."

As time passed, and the cocoon continued slowly to clear, she could now finally see J inside it. "J, J, come back to me." Exhausted, she called out over and over. "Come on," she cried, "come on." She laid her head down on the cocoon and unconsciously started beating on it. She reared up when she heard a cracking sound.

"Oh no," she said, as she alternately patted and pulled at the growing crack. "J, tell me what to do," she pleaded.

Suddenly, the cocoon fell completely open, and she heard J heave a loud sigh. She sat back on her heels and just stared at him.

She blinked as he opened his eyes and looked up at her.

"Got any water?" he croaked.

"Don't you dare do that again, okay? For a minute there, I thought I was losing you."

She turned to get some water for them both.

He gave her a big smile and simply said, "Thank you for my life."

Alexis smiled back and said, "You're welcome."

Startled, J pushed himself up into a seated position, then he looked around, surprised to find himself in a cave. The last thing he remembered was the pain as he hit the water.

Alexis looked critically at him. "You scared me." She pulled the water bottles over and passed one to J. Looking closely at him, she tried to analyze what was different. Then she saw most of his hair was falling out. She picked it up and showed him. Jon stared. His hands went to his head and more fell out. He felt bumps protruding from the back of his head. He paled as the implications staggered him. His father had gone through the same thing when his grandfather died.

"No, oh, no," he pleaded. *Please, let my father still be alive,* he prayed. His next thought was maybe his father was sick or something. *Please, just let him not be able to administer his job because he is sick, not dead.*

He didn't want to think what it all meant. He was frantic with worry—not just about his father but his entire family. Were they hidden? He had to get to his home world. Jon knew Dr. Michaels didn't know who he was or anything about him. She had risked her life saving him. He owed her so much, so he pushed his pain and worry for his family into the back of his mind to be dealt with later.

"Can you explain all this?" She gestured to the broken cocoon and the clumps of hair.

"Not all of it. I can't, not right now. I can't tell you a lot."

It was his turn to blush as he felt his head and the areas that earlier had healing scabs on them. His skin was unmarked and smooth.

"I can speculate, but I have not observed the phenomenon in a long time. The scabs are common in my family and usually form on small hurts. This is the first time I have seen them on large wounds. That was really kind of interesting." He added, with a twinkle in his eye, "Maybe we won't need doctors."

She glared as she patted him on the arm, then turned away from him

"Whoa, there. I was just kidding," Jon said.

"By the way, my first name is Alexis. Just thought you should know. We were told to call you J, but I'm sure you have a real name."

She realized she was attracted to him for several reasons. He seemed kind and courageous, although she didn't really know much about him. She only had her gut feelings to go on, but the prefect hated him, so it intrigued her. She wanted to know more about him.

"Let me introduce myself. I'm Jon-Tor, from the planet Tyrea. Please, just call me Jon."

"I am exhausted, and I have been beating on your cocoon for hours. I'm relieved that you are out of it. It jolted me when it formed."

She reached for the supplies and, rummaging for a while, finally found the bio-scanner. "Thank you, Sue," she said quietly, as she turned back to her patient, ready to help in whatever way she could.

CHAPTER 8

Prefect Tamias of Tyrea was not happy. He shrieked at his soldiers, he yelled at the doctors and nurses on duty, and he especially bellowed at Warden Skinner.

"You told me that this facility had top-notch security and look what happened. You lost my prisoner. I want a thorough search of the hospital but also the surrounding land. You, sir, are a fool, and you have a traitor among you. We restrained him. Someone had to have taken off those restraints. He couldn't do that for himself. He was supposed to be sedated. He's gone, which proves he wasn't sedated, was he? You just let him walk out of here. He was hurt in the crash, but, apparently, not as critical as your doctor thought. What kind of people would let this happen?" He bellowed on and on.

Warden Skinner just stood there, but the skin on his neck kept getting redder and redder. He wished this pompous personage would leave as he had planned, but now that would not happen unless he could produce the prisoner.

"Find Dr. Michaels," he demanded of the nearest doctor. The woman hurried out. Soon she was back with the report that it was Dr. Michaels' day off.

The prefect turned his disdainful stare on the warden. "Well, that's convenient, isn't it? Anyone else have a day off, too? Maybe they are all together playing cards somewhere."

"This is a large facility, Prefect. Many people have the day off or are on vacation."

The prefect just stared at him accusatively.

This was his well-run facility. "Prefect, perhaps you can answer a few of *my* questions. You are here demanding procedures and actions of *my* staff, while providing no information about a potentially dangerous person, including his name. What do you say for yourself, sir?"

"You need no more information. Well, send people to check on them," he yelled in the warden's face. "I hold you personally responsible for this fiasco."

The warden turned away from him and walked back to his office, with the prefect following closely. There, he called the Air Patrol Office and explained about the missing prisoner.

"They asked for a description." He looked at the prefect, who just shook his head.

"They need some kind of description. You can't ask them to find someone with nothing to go on."

But the prefect was beyond paranoid and refused to add any more. "Just find him," he demanded. "Some men can search around the prison."

Warren Skinner gave the Air Patrol a very general description of the prisoner's physical appearance and hung up. Turning to the prefect, he informed him, "I already have my staff searching the prison and our grounds for your man. I have none to spare for an additional search outside the walls. Besides, I doubt he'd be able to escape these walls. He was badly hurt. He is probably hiding in one of the many storage closets."

"Well, give me some of your air cars and my men can search," he demanded, as he stormed away from the desk.

"You can have *one* air car," the warden told the prefect, whose facial features had turned thunderous as he slammed the door on his way out. He called the garage to give the order that one air car, and only one air car, would be available to the prefect and his men to use in their search, and then he rang his secretary to get a copy of the staffing for the day.

"Could this day get any worse?"

The warden's secretary hurried in with a printout of all employees with the day off or those who were on vacation. He signaled the Air Patrol Office and relayed the list to them. He couldn't wait to end the whole thing and for the high and mighty prefect of Tyrea to be gone, prisoner or no prisoner.

CHAPTER 9

Staking out the prison and hospital, Phillip saw a man hurrying toward the hospital. He didn't know Lu-zan, but he was sure this must be him. Matt O'Shea had sent the name of the person they were to expect but did not provide a description. Phillip's friend had come through with a description of the IPS representative. He needed to catch him before anyone from the prison saw him. All hell would break out if the warden or prefect knew about the crim-scan. The prefect and warden would comb the prison, and they might not think of Dr. Michaels. It was her day off. Phillip wondered whether they would think her innocent with the prisoner gone at the same time. At least she had an excuse. She frequently sought solitude on her days off.

"Hey, Lu-zan. Hold on, man, wait for me," Phillip called out to him.

Lu-zan stopped with a puzzled expression on his face as he turned to face Phillip.

"What? Who are...?" Lu-zan asked, just as Phillip reached them.

"How did you get here so fast? I wasn't expecting you until tomorrow." Phillip spoke to cover Lu-zan's exclamation. His arm went around Lu-zan's shoulders as he whispered, "Dr. Michaels sent me."

Lu-zan bowed to him and offered his hand. Phillip shook hands and gave him a wide grin.

"Come, my wife and kids are eagerly waiting for you. They can't wait to go camping," Phillip said easily, as he glanced at the prison entrance and saw the warden watching. He led Lu-zan away toward his air car. Lu-zan smiled and played along, and the warden seemed satisfied.

In the mid-sized air car, Phillip sighed in relief. Before he could explain, Lu-zan glared at him and demanded to know what was going on.

"We got J out, but he is still in danger. The Prefect of Tyrea is searching for him. The prefect has tied the warden's hands since he arrived. I can take you to J, but we have to be careful. I'm on Dr. Michaels' team. We are being followed and our houses, searched. It has been hard on all of us."

"Are we being followed now?" Lu-zan asked.

Phillip looked around. "I don't know, but I don't think so."

"Fly us to your home and get your family. I think if we act like old friends that visit, we'll be okay. You can show us where we are going to camp. Yes?" Lu-zan surveyed the area outside the windows to observe whether they were being followed.

"Should I just fly around a little first to lose any tail? By the way, are you allergic to dogs or anything?"

"No, we shouldn't fly around seemingly aimlessly because we want to appear normal and not suspicious. It would appear very suspicious if you deviated too much from your normal routine. And no, I'm not allergic to dogs. I love dogs. What kind do you have?"

"It's an unusual breed called a Ta ashi no tomodachi, which means multi-legged friend. I got it as a Christmas present for the kids. Great watch dog, especially being on a prison planet. I thought it was an excellent protection for the family, and that breed really loves children."

"I have heard of that breed. What did you name it?" Lu-zan inquired.

"We just call him Ashi for short. Easier for the kids to say. He's the reason for the extra-large air car. Ashi is the size of a miniature horse—and strong. The kids ride him around the yard."

The first thing Lu-zan saw after they landed was a small mountain of flying fur coming toward them. Phillip stepped out, putting his hand up, and the dog skidded to a smooth stop in front of him. Two small children slid off Ashi's back to the ground and grabbed onto Phillip's legs, laughing. All six of Ashi's legs were moving, but he stayed in one place in front of Phillip. Phillip's wife and an older boy, who looked like a smaller version of Phillip, came walking up to greet the guests. When Phillip gave the signal to Ashi that it was okay to move, the dog moved in an undulating pattern that reminded Lu-zan of a swirling wash mop.

"Let's get our camping gear, and we can talk while we eat lunch," Mari, Phillip's wife, said, as she started moving toward the house. The two younger children came running up to Ashi, who flopped down so they could climb onto him, and they went running back toward the house. Lu-zan watched, amazed, as the dog moved so smoothly with his charges onboard.

Everyone helped with carrying food and supplies out to the picnic table and settled down to eat. Phillip introduced his wife and children, who were so excited to meet someone new. The dog ran from one person to the next person, not sure who was giving the best rubs or treats.

"Are Dr. Michaels and Jon very far away from here?" Lu-zan rubbed the dog's belly as he waited.

"So that's his name. The prefect wouldn't tell us his real name. He just said to call him 'J.' No, they are close to the prison in a cave, and that's part of the problem. The concealed cave is fairly large, but Jon was in a cocoon, and we couldn't move him very far. I didn't see it happen, but when we lowered Jon into the river that runs under the prison, he had a reaction, and the result was the cocoon material that formed around him. I scouted out a kind of hidey-hole that Dr. Michaels and Jon can get to if someone stumbles onto the cave. We had stocked the cave with provisions as a temporary stop, but now I don't know about moving Jon."

"Jon's in a cocoon?" Lu-zan anxiously asked. "We can talk later. Okay, are we actually going to camp?"

"Yes, I thought we could take the family and get fairly close. You and I can go explore, and I would guide you to the cave. Ashi can play with the kids while Mari sets up." Ashi's ears perked up when he heard his name. Phillip automatically reached over and scratched his ears.

"That plan has merit, but I dislike endangering your wife and children in this. Ashi, while a great dog, doesn't seem like much protection."

"No? Just watch. Ashi, GUARD." Ashi immediately stopped playing and scanned the area intently. Not seeing anything, he herded the children together into a circle where he guarded them as he continued scanned the surrounding area, including watching the sky.

"I have seen him take on a wombear. It looks like a cross between a small brown bear and a wombat from Earth. The wombear was twice his size, but he herded it away like he was herding sheep. What a sight to see! The wombear could have killed him, but it seemed to want to get away from a more dangerous animal."

"Well," said Lu-zan, "I feel better knowing he'll be around."

"My wife and I have always enjoyed camping. It's an incredibly beautiful planet. We're lucky our kids also love to camp. As long as the kids don't see Dr. Michaels and Jon, they should be safe while we're gone. I thought we would go to the Emil National Forest on the plateau above the falls. It's close to the prison, but not too close. The family has often gone there. It shouldn't seem out of place to show it to you, and it has a great fishing hole. It surprised me to see you were alone. I was expecting someone named Matt to come, too."

"Matt needs to oversee the main attack area. We lost a lot of good people, so Matt is there. Do you have a map of the area?"

Phillip activated his three-dimensional map to bring up the area. He handed out drinks to all while Lu-zan studied the map.

While Ashi kept the children occupied, Phillip, Mari, and Lu-zan talked about the plan.

"We need to consider possibilities in case Jon is still in a cocoon or cannot walk. He will probably need help. Do we have an anti-gravity disc with us?" Lu-zan asked.

"Yes, we do," Phillip informed him.

Mari fixed them a meal fit for a king, with fresh fruit from their orchard and vegetables from their garden. Ashi whined and made everyone give him a piece. Phillip stated that he earns it because he's still a growing boy. Lu-zan eyed some of the unfamiliar fruit askance, but Mari laughed and showed him how to eat it. His delighted look of pleased surprise made everyone laugh.

"Can we pack some of these, too?" Lu-zan asked longingly.

"I'm sure we can squeeze a few into the pack," Mari assured him with a smile.

Phillip and Mari divided tasks and quickly gathered camping equipment, clothes, and food.

The next morning, as they were packing the air car, an Air Patrol car came by and stopped. Lu-zan tensed up, but Phillip signaled to let him handle it.

"Phillip," the patrolman called from the air car.

"Stone, what brings you here?" Phillip asked, as he walked out of the house.

From his vantage point by the window, Lu-zan noticed that Ashi was jumping around with his tail wagging. Phillip greeted his friend as he landed the patrol air car.

"The warden is in an uproar because a prisoner escaped. Have you seen anyone who doesn't belong around here? Anything suspicious?" He reached up to pat Ashi's head.

Lu-zan came out of the house carrying some blankets, and the patrolman eyed him suspiciously.

"Stone, meet Lu-zan, who is joining us on a camping trip. We're going to show him some of our beautiful scenery. Been telling him for years to come, and he finally made it."

"Do you have a description?" Lu-zan asked, as he piled the blankets on the bedding pile.

"That's the strange thing. We don't know exactly what he looks like except he is very tall. He escaped and may be with someone who works at the prison. Phillip, I'm sorry, but orders are orders. You work at the prison, but this gentleman doesn't fit the description."

"That's okay, man. You're just doing your job. Just to let you know, in case you're asked, we plan to show my friend the Emil National Forest."

Stone smiled. "You will love it up there. It's so beautiful. I appreciate the update. See you later, and have a pleasant stay." He shook everyone's hands again and petted Ashi before he got into his patrol car.

The family and Lu-zan finished packing the air car, and after taking off, headed in the opposite direction, toward the forest. Phillip flew in a spiral up to the plateau. Phillip said, "He is a good man."

Everyone heaved a sigh of relief. Ashi kept sticking his head out of the window, with his tongue hanging out, making the family laugh. Lu-zan looked at the majestic scenery and the beautiful falls in the distance. Towering above the falls was the prison, with a dark and brooding presence. It sat like a monstrous toad among the beautiful trees and hills. He shuddered, thinking of Jon in that place. He turned to Phillip to further discuss ideas to transport Jon and Dr. Michaels, but with the children staring at them from their seats, he changed his mind.

Phillip landed the air car in a beautiful clearing with a small stream. The excited kids were jumping up and down.

"All right, everyone, grab a pack and disembark." Phillip matched his actions to his words and was the first one off. Mari turned to help with the packs and supplies she had packed. Ashi barked in excitement and bounced around everyone.

"Hey, Lu-zan, come help me set up the tents. Come on, kids, where do you want your tent?" Phillip yelled to the kids.

Mari laughed at him. "You don't need any help. Those tents set themselves up. Let Ashi help you."

"Ha ha." Phillip turned and grinned.

It wasn't long before the tents were up, and Mari was fixing lunch for everyone. Lu-zan kept an eager eye on her unpacking. Mari hid a smile as she pulled out the fruit that he liked so well.

"Wow, this is great," Lu-zan exclaimed, as he sat down to eat. The kids and Ashi came running, laughing that Lu-zan was going to eat all the food. Lu-zan mock-grabbed at them, setting them off again on a giggling fit, and Ashi barked, wanting to be grabbed at, too.

Lu-zan looked over the campsite as he again sat down to eat. The oldest son especially impressed him with his air of maturity and how he watched his younger siblings. Lu-zan watched him as he kept an eye on his father. Phillip made sure all his children were included equally in both work and play according to age and abilities. The son, being just twelve years of age, was at that stage of growth where he was growing taller but was still thin. In a couple of years, he would probably be taller than his father.

He approved the way Phillip made sure the tent for the kids and Ashi was between Lu-zan's tent and their parent's tent. There was a stream nearby, and the ground was flat and free of debris. It was an excellent location.

After lunch, all the kids, with the dog in tow, went off to fish with Mari. The men gathered together to make plans. Then Phillip sat down with a couple of fishing poles and a tackle box and worked at readying the poles, checking gear, and offering different lures to Lu-zan.

"What's this?" Lu-zan looked the gear over.

"Well, I figure it wouldn't hurt to have camouflage ready, just in case a patrol came by. That prefect was one scary dude, and I wouldn't put it past him to be watching the area around the prison. I bet we'll get company soon."

Lu-zan continued an ongoing conversation he and Matt had before he left. "We have to get an idea how to get Jon to his home world of Tyrea. An Intergalactic Training ship landing at the spaceport on Tyrea would be very conspicuous. Even getting into orbit would be tricky. Maybe the best idea is to have them travel there on a commercial vessel," he informed Phillip.

"You mean Jon needs to go to Tyrea? That prefect sure wants him to go to Tyrea. Why would he travel where he would be a prisoner or killed?"

Lu-zan tried to explain without revealing too much. "Jon is important to Tyrea, and we think there is an attempt going on to overthrow the government. He needs to return."

"I packed my link in my pack. We can check ships going out. I know the prefect said he was leaving today on a ship. Maybe you can get him on a ship going to another planet and then connect to a flight to Tyrea," Phillip suggested.

Lu-zan grinned. "That's good thinking, Phillip. Maybe we should give you a job as a covert agent."

An hour later, Lu-zan was fishing with the help of Ashi, who waited hopefully, even if he caught nothing. The kids were playing a board game with their parents when an air car appeared from the west, and Ashi started running toward Phillip.

"Company's coming," Phillip called, as he got up to greet the visitors. He signaled Ashi to go on alert.

"Who are you? Why are you in this area?" a gruff voice reverberated across the clearing. "You need to leave at once."

"The Air Patrol has cleared us to be here," Phillip replied to the descending air car, and Ashi growled low in his throat. Phillip signaled for him to stay by him. Ashi stared at the men and bared his teeth.

"You need to leave now. We don't care what those guys told you."

"And you are?"

"We are from the prison. Leave now."

Lu-zan moved to stand next to Phillip, adding his support in case the confrontation turned ugly. Mari had gathered the children together and was ushering them to their tents. Phillip signaled for Ashi to guard the kids. The dog took off like a rocket, standing guard in front of Mari and the kids.

"Hey, I remember you guys. You were with the prefect of Tyrea, and some of you were in the crash. Are you feeling better now?" Phillip asked in a friendly voice. "What are you doing out here?"

"The prefect wants the area inspected for an escaped prisoner, so you need to leave or we'll have to arrest you. And since you work at the prison hospital, we need you to come with us. NOW."

"I'm on vacation with my family, and they have cleared us to be here. Check with Air Patrol Authority."

"We don't have to check with anyone else. Stretch out on the ground. We are taking you all in for obstructing justice and especially *you*," he said, indicating Phillip, "for questioning."

Everyone tensed as they readied themselves for the battle to take place. Phillip looked helplessly at his family, not sure what else to do. Ashi took an attack position and growled loudly. Another voice sounded across the clearing.

"Attention unidentified aircraft. You have no authority to patrol this area. Identify yourselves."

The men twirled toward the unfamiliar voice. "The prefect of Tyrea and the warden at the prison gave us authority to search this area."

"Well, you'd better double check that order, because they do not have that authority. They need to apply for permission from the Air Patrol Authority. I already cleared this group, and if you want no more trouble than you are already in, then clear out and leave law-abiding citizens alone."

Ashi moved to within a distance that he could jump and attack easily and growled even louder.

The prefect's men looked uneasy, with quick glances at the large animal.

"Better go, before I call the entire Air Patrol up here, or the dog attacks. Believe me, you don't want either kind of trouble."

With a lot of muttering and angry glances, the prison air car lifted and moved off in the prison's direction. Everyone breathed a sigh of relief. Phillip signaled for Ashi to stand down and gave him lots of petting and approval. He even produced a treat from his pocket.

"I saw them moving in your direction from Bellows Falls and thought I should run interference. Those soldiers are causing trouble all over. Are you all okay?"

"Stone, you are a lifesaver. They wanted to arrest us! They said they were going to arrest me, my entire family, and my friend, too. What's this world coming to? We were only fishing. We have some fish left. Do you want some? It's fantastic. Mari cooked it."

"Well, if Mari fixed it, okay. I know you can't cook worth shit," Stone joked as hpetted Ashi.

"Come on, I'll get you some. Did you find that prisoner yet?"

"No, not yet. Honestly, I think he's probably hiding somewhere in the prison or something, but we have to check."

"Sure, you have to do your job and keep everyone safe. Here you go, best fish ever," Phillip said, with pride in his voice. "Can my kids fish or can my kids fish?"

"Mmm, your kids can fish. This is wonderful. Mari, what magic was used to make this fish taste so good? You having a good time?" Obviously enjoying the unexpected treat, he finished up the last of the fish and vegetables.

"Yes, sir," the kids danced around him, grinning.

"Seriously, you all be careful. If that prisoner is loose, he might be dangerous. That idiot warden might let those guards patrol again. They are a nasty bunch. I might not be around next time if any of you got hurt," he said theatrically. "It was very nice to meet you." He shook hands with Lu-zan. "Hope you enjoy our beautiful planet." He waved as he took off in his air car.

Lu-zan said, so everyone could hear, "Like you said, a good man."

They packed dark clothes and needed supplies into backpacks as the men got ready to leave. After the earlier incident, they didn't want to take any chances. Lu-zan cringed when he thought about the confrontation that had occurred earlier. At least it had not escalated because of the quick actions of Stone and Ashi. One good friend and an incredible dog—a brilliant combination to have in a tough situation. Extracting Jon from this situation would only be harder if they got into a messy tangle with pseudo-military types.

Thinking about that, a rough voice surprised Lu-zan. "Now we can get down to business."

Phillip yelled at Ashi, as the dog dashed at the men who materialized out of the trees. Ashi attacked the first man, growling and covering ground at an amazing speed. The man yelped and fired at the dog. Ashi swerved to the side and kept swiftly covering ground toward the attacking men running from the trees. One man targeted the dog and fired a killing shot. Ashi bit the first man just as the shot rang out. Man and dog both went down. Ashi had bitten the man as Phillip came running up. Phillip saw the attacker sight on Lu-zan, who was grappling with one man. He picked up a nearby rock and threw it at him. The man flinched away and then turned to aim at Phillip. Though Ashi was dead, he still gripped the attacker's leg in his teeth. The man pulled a knife to cut the dog's teeth from him, but Phillip caught his arm, stopping him. The man slashed at Phillip, catching him in the side.

Before the attacker by the trees could pull the trigger, Stone shot him down. A voice came from the sky, causing everyone to freeze.

"Put down the guns. NOW," Stone thundered from the air car.

Startled, they looked up and saw that an Air Patrol car had ballooned open and now revealed two side wings of guns pointed at them. Silently, the two remaining attackers moved off into the forest, one of them limping badly.

Mari ran after the children as they dashed toward their father and Ashi. She grabbed the two younger ones and turned them into her shoulder to shield them from the sight.

Phillip struggled to gain his feet, but his wound prevented him from moving far. He crawled to the side of Ashi. He looked back at Mari and shook his head no. His oldest son ran to his side to help and skidded to a halt as he viewed all the blood oozing from his father's side as Phillip cradled Ashi's body.

Stone landed the Air Patrol car and ran to help. Lu-zan also ran to stand guard over the downed soldier still attached to Ashi and tangled with Phillip. He kicked the knife out of the screaming man's hand and wrestled his arms to his side.

Stone reported to headquarters, asking for aid, and to start the search for the attackers. "Put pressure on that slash to stop the bleeding," he ordered Lu-zan, who hastened to follow his orders.

"Phillip, did you recognize any of the attackers?" Stone asked.

Phillip looked up at Stone. "I think if you check your recording of your previous visit, you will find this was the same group," he replied, as he grimaced in pain.

"I need to verify first. Lu-zan, do you know how to do a field dressing?"

"Yes, throw me the pack."

Stone threw him the Emergency Med Pack and reported and verified the information on the recording.

Phillip smiled at his son. "Good job. Watch Lu-zan do the dressing and learn. It just proves you never know when you might need the knowledge." When he lay back on the ground, his hand went to Ashi's fur to offer a silent farewell and gratitude to a gallant member of his family.

CHAPTER 10

Minister Wayne was worried. He had received no word or communication from Tariq in months. He hoped the other minister would have some ideas on dealing with Tariq.

Minister Zikri Truli came in a few minutes later, making a grand entrance as usual.

"What do you need, my dear fellow?" he said, as he fluffed his long hair.

"Zackari is missing. Do you know anything about where he went? He was supposed to go to the capital and check on Tariq, but no one has seen him."

"Why should I care what Zackari is doing?" Zikri protested.

"You should care because we sent him there. We need to know what is happening with Tariq. Zackari was your choice of whom to send. Tariq is power hungry, and I wouldn't put it past him to have reacted badly when Zackari showed up. Tariq is not responding to my calls, and we need to know what's happening."

"Okay, okay, I'll send someone to discreetly investigate." Zikri yawned in weariness and plumped his hair.

"See that you do that as soon as possible," Wayne said angrily.

Zikri strolled out of Wayne's office and leisurely returned to his own. There, he wasted no time in sending his own man to the capital to find out what was happening. This ruse he was playing was wearing thin. He really was not sure how much longer he could keep it. He'd started this concealment when he noticed how Zackari and Wayne were becoming even more aggressive in their methods in dealing with the king. He had suggested that Zackari be sent to Tariq in order to gather more information on his true ambitions. Zikri knew that few people remembered that he and his family were related to the king. He needed more information if he were to protect the king.

CHAPTER 11

It did not please the prefect when the guards reported back that they could not search outside the prison fences. He couldn't speak because he was shaking with rage. The guards eased back. They knew from experience how violent he could become. All the current guards had scars from the prefect's past rages.

The warden and his staff waited to see what the man would do. In fact, the pompous prefect exhausted the warden, and he couldn't wait to see the backside of him.

"Anything wrong?" the warden asked. He watched as the prefect achieved a remarkable shade of red, which was approaching an interesting shade of purple. Maybe he could take pity on the man—then the prefect actually sputtered.

"I'm sorry, I didn't catch that. Why don't you sit down and get a glass of water? It might help. You really are a remarkable shade of red. You don't want to have a stoke, do you?"

"What do you mean, we can't search outside the prison? I asked *you* about searching the lands outside."

"I beg your pardon, you didn't, actually. We searched inside the prison and our grounds within our walls. You DEMANDED that I give you use of one of our air cars. I did and then called the Air Patrol for you."

"You, you, you idiot! Why would I want an air car except to search outside the walls? Answer me that, you imbecile."

In a remarkably calm voice, the warden responded.

"Prefect, you should have talked about that with the Air Patrol Command. Since your prisoner is not on prison grounds, you no longer have a reason to be here. I sincerely suggest you leave and take your guards with you. Your presence here disrupts the smooth running of MY prison. GUARDS! Please escort the prefect off the premises."

"BUT IT'S YOUR RESPONSIBILITY TO HELP ME FIND MY PRISONER," the prefect screamed at the warden as he stared around at the approaching guards. "STOP THEM, FOOLS!" he screeched at his own guards.

"Oh, but that's where you are wrong. Once my search showed no prisoner hiding within its walls or on prison grounds, my responsibility was over. My authority does not extend outside those perimeters. The Air Patrol handles the investigation outside the prison grounds. I suggest you take the matter up with them. It seems your soldiers have shot one of our citizens and killed his dog. They will charge you for what your guards have done, and I'm sure you will never be able to land here again. The guards will escort you out."

He turned and walked away with a satisfyingly warm spot over his heart. The prefect didn't see his smile. He was way too busy protesting being manhandled by the guards.

The prefect's guards reluctantly left, followed closely by the prison guards out of the prison. He shouted dire consequences to everyone the whole way.

Warden Skinner heard one guard to say, "I wanted to open a bar, anyway."

The prison guards came back with smirks on their faces. Spontaneous applause came from everybody they passed. They had initially felt sorry for the guards, but they had showed themselves to be bullies.

CHAPTER 12

Wheeling from what she had learned from Tariq, the queen stumbled down the hallway. She didn't understand what was happening.

"My lady, are you alright? Let me help you." Willem caught up with her and gently took her arm.

"Don't touch me!"

She wheeled away from him in fear and revulsion of the uniform. She continued trying to walk anywhere to get away from the hated uniform. Flashes of Tariq and one of his soldier's hands holding her down and digging into her shoulder to get the disc screamed across her thoughts. Battling tears, the grief and rage Tariq had caused blinded her as she stumbled.

"I am your friend, my lady. Please trust me. Let me get you somewhere Tariq can't use you against your family, your world. Don't let him win, my lady. Please let me help you," Willem said, as he slowly followed her convoluted trail down the hall.

She squinted at the man. This time she saw the boy who used to play with her sons in the hallways or in the family's quarters. But now, he wore the uniform of the man who had killed the king, her husband, her love. Hate rose in her throat. "You traitor. You work for that monster!" She turned away from him.

"My lady, they hurt you. Let me get you sanctuary, and where we can treat your wounds. I promise to tell you why I wear this uniform."

She eyed him suspiciously. She knew she could not go far without help. *Oh, Borig, I don't see what to do. Who can I trust?* she thought.

"May I get help for you, my lady? If you don't trust me, let me get someone you trust to help you."

"I don't know who to trust," she murmured.

"My parents have been loyal to you and King Borig their entire lives. Let me get them," he pleaded.

"NO! I don't want to endanger anyone else."

"My Queen, they hurt you. Trust someone, and I am already here. Trust me. I pledge on my life to do my best to keep you safe." He stood tall before her and quietly waited for her decision.

"All right. I put my life in your hands," she said, as she realized she had to trust someone.

It overwhelmed Willem with gratitude, and he hastened to support her.

"Prince Jon and I used to hide in hidey-holes. Do you know of one where you could lie down?" he asked, as he tried to move her forward as fast as he could. Meeting anyone in the halls would elicit many questions.

The queen made a turn to the right, which took them toward her quarters. They hurried into a reception area that was dedicated to the beautiful local artwork.

"Here, it's here," she told him, as she scanned the floor.

Willem looked around in confusion as he looked for an obvious hidey-hole. *I see nothing that would be useful,* he thought. *My brain is a muddle. It wouldn't be obvious. Look closer.* Willem looked over at the queen and noticed she was scrutinizing the floor. He moved closer to watch where she was looking.

"Is the hidey-hole under the floor?"

"Yes, search for the seam. I know it's in this corner," she said in a tired voice.

"My lady, please sit and rest. I will look for you."

She sent him a grateful smile as she sat down on a chair and cradled her injured arm to her.

Willem bent to inspect the seams, following the lines to see any gaps. The highly polished and tightly spaced floorboards caused him to make a more scrupulous inspection of the area. He looked at an area where the seam seemed to separate slightly, almost invisible.

As he ran his finger along the seam, the queen whispered, "Did you find it?"

"I think so. It's so small," he whispered back, as he got his knife out to pry the board. It was easier than he thought it would be, and the edge of the board slid out of its groove. After that, it was easy to remove the section of boards covering the opening. "That's really ingenious," he murmured.

"Yes, it is," she murmured back.

He got down into the hole and used his wrist-light to inspect the area. The queen waited anxiously.

"It looks large enough and has a curve into an alcove. Do you want to stay here or look for another?"

I think I should do this now. I'm so tired, she thought. "I'll stay down there and hopefully be unnoticed."

He helped her down into the hole and to the little alcove.

"I'll go get you some supplies, and any food I can find. My lady, I'll do my best to get help for you as soon as possible."

He turned to go but stopped and gave her the penlight. He hurried up into the rooms and grabbed whatever he could find to give her some comfort. Luckily, he found a kitchen area with water and food, but, before he could gather anything more, he heard footsteps. Two soldiers in Tariq uniforms came around the corner.

"What are you doing?" they demanded.

"I'm hungry," he answered. One soldier looked into the large sack and snatched it from his hands. "Hey, that's mine," he yelled.

"Carry on," the soldier told him, as the two men pushed past him.

He found another large cloth bag and quickly packed it full. He also gave her a knife to open stubborn packages, and in dire need, defend herself. On the way back, he grabbed pillows and blankets. He carried everything back to her, where he made a comfortable area so she could lie down, and he had grabbed some of the beautiful pillows to add to her comfort. He also put a low stool he had spied near her so she would have a place for her water and food.

"My lady, I'm sorry, but I need to put a pressure pack against your wound to help stop the loss of blood."

She nodded reluctantly and bared her shoulder so he could work. It was soon done, and she gratefully pulled her clothes over her shoulder again.

"I must leave you now. Stay quiet and use the wrist-light only a little. I'll return as soon as possible." He left her and replaced the boards carefully, so the seam was barely noticeable.

CHAPTER 13

The impromptu team of Lu-zan, Phillip, and his son made good time considering Phillip's injury. They stopped several times for breaks and for Phillip to check directions. The forest had little undergrowth, but with the growing darkness, Phillip was having trouble reading the compass. The wrist-light supplied by Lu-zan helped. He made frequent checks of the compass and made slight adjustments to their heading. The forest was mostly species of Earth-like tree growth, including tall oaks, maples, and a few evergreens, mixed in with many species from other planets. Lu-zan noted the lack of rocks and debris on the forest floor.

Lu-zan had updated Matt on the attack at the campsite, and the injuries and loss the family had sustained. He also told him that the cave was very close to the prison. Phillip proved to be a skilled tracker, and his son was a great help to Phillip when he became fatigued. After a small amount of backtracking, they finally came into view of the cave. Phillip, sore and tired, was happy to have made such good time. It pleased Lu-zan they had made good progress across the rolling hillside, especially through a forest. They had used little light except to check the compass, and the lack of undergrowth in this forest helped them. Lu-zan wondered what this forest would look like in the daytime. Too bad they were seeing it at night, he thought. Visibility was maybe five feet, so Lu-zan stayed very close to Phillip and his son for the entire trip.

"I'll go in first. Dr. Michaels might be startled if Jon is still in the cocoon, or they might be sleeping."

"Okay, be careful. I'll wait a few minutes, but don't take too long. I'm rather eager to see Jon for myself," Lu-zan stated.

Phillip entered and turned on the flashlight once he was out of sight of the cave opening.

"Alexis," he called softly. A slight noise reached his ear, and he slowed and called again.

Abruptly, a face appeared in the beam. It was bald and had dyed blue eyelids. "Yak...what?" he cried.

"Phillip?" came a calm voice.

"Dr. Michaels!" Phillip yelled to cover how startled he felt. "Are you alright?"

Alexis ducked around Jon and squinted as she faced the beam of the flashlight. "Could you lower that a little? Phillip, this is Jon. He doesn't quite look like he did. The cocoon changed something in him. Are you here by yourself? Didn't Matt O'Shea come with you?"

"Lu-zan is here. Matt had to cover the original attack site. I left him outside. Let me go get him," he told her, as he hastened to the cave entrance. He shook his head as he sought to get his heartbeat back to normal.

Alexis and Jon moved back and lit more lanterns. They moved supplies around to make room. The three men came into the inner cave. They all stared at Jon, for none could understand or believe the changes that had occurred. Jon waited nervously for his friend to acknowledge that it was really him. He started to speak and stopped.

It came to Lu-zan that Jon was unsure of his reception. He moved forward and took the young man into his arms. The movement broke the tension that had developed in the cave. Jon grabbed onto Lu-zan and held on like his life depended on the contact. Alexis watched the reunion silently.

"What did you do to yourself? At least the new haircut suits you," Lu-zan joked to break the tension, and he patted Jon's shoulder. Jon broke off from Lu-zan and wiped his eyes.

"Don't hug him so hard. We just got him healed up," Alexis complained.

"Man, I'm so glad to see you guys. Do you have a plan for us?" Jon asked hopefully, as he looked at Lu-zan.

"Us?" Lu-zan asked in confusion. "Is Dr. Michaels coming, too?"

"I'm sorry, I assumed." Jon turned to Alexis and asked, "Do you want to come?" He left unsaid, "With me?"

Alexis hesitated as she considered what she would be leaving. *I have a job here, but I had been wanting to explore my options.* Indecision ruled her as she looked at Phillip and Jon. *This could get very dangerous. Do I want to put myself in that kind of danger?* She weighed her obligations to the prison and her obligation to Jon as his doctor. *We have talked about Jon's family, and I think I understand, at least a little, what Jon is facing.* In the end, she decided she wanted to be part of this.

"I'm coming with you," she told Jon. Jon's smile was her answer. She turned to Lu-zan and said, "Hello, I'm Dr. Alexis Michaels. Please call me Alexis."

"Alexis, I am very pleased to meet you. Phillip had high praise, and I have some need of your skills. The prefect's men attacked us at the campsite. They injured Phillip, and they killed their wonderful guard dog, Ashi. We need to move to make it back to the campsite by dawn. As Jon's doctor, is he fit enough to travel fast through heavy forest?" Lu-zan asked anxiously.

Jon started to answer, but Lu-zan's hand on his arm stopped him, and he also turned to look at Alexis.

"It's hard to know for sure since I only have my emergency medical bag with me, but I think Jon's okay. He's still sore and lacking vitality, but with our help, I think he'll make it. He has undergone physical changes, such as hair loss and a ridge going down his back, and some skull abnormalities. I don't understand what those mean yet. It was scary. I still don't know what the cocoon was, but when Jon came out of it, he didn't have the visible scars he had before. I tried to palpate the areas of the worst injuries, and they seemed to have healed. When I get to some deep scan medical equipment, like a CT scanner or an x-ray, I will feel better. As for Phillip, let me examine him and see if he can travel."

During the entire time she was talking, Jon watched her. He reached for her hand, and she let him. Phillip and Lu-zan exchanged looks. Maybe that's the way it is. *Good,* thought Lu-zan.

"We need you to hide from the younger children. I think Stone will probably take Ashi as evidence of the attack. You are going to love Mari. She is very special." Lu-zan continued. "The kids are young. Phillip's eldest son is here to help, too," he added, as he put his hand on the young man's shoulder. "He has been a great help. Jon, can we talk privately somewhere? I have important news."

"Sure, come this way." Jon sent Alexis a last look as he led Lu-zan to the entrance of the cave.

"Jon…Jon, I don't know how to tell you this."

"What is it?"

"Jon, all hell is breaking loose on your home planet. Your family is in danger, and unexplained disappearances have occurred. So far, the list includes your father, your mother, sister, and two brothers, plus various ministers. The government claims a series of unusual freak accidents. General Tariq demands to know your location." With each word uttered by Lu-zan, Jon turned into himself, seeming to grow smaller and smaller as his grief threatened to crush what little control he had left.

Jon's grief-filled face turned from Lu-zan to look at the forest. An oppressive scent of pine teased the air as Lu-zan, equally worried and haggard, wondered how to tell him all that had happened in his home world. He took a breath and plunged ahead.

"But it goes further than that. We cannot contact any of your living relatives at all. We can't get any information on the condition of your father. He has disappeared, and General Tariq claims to know nothing of his whereabouts. You're the last one in your entire family, and now someone wants you. Why, Jon? Can you tell me what's going on?" Lu-zan pleaded, wanting to know how to best help his friend.

Placing a comforting touch on Jon's shoulder, Lu-zan could see the shimmer of tears and feel the tension in his friend's body.

"Jon, do you know what's going on?" he gently asked again.

"All of them, gone? I felt my father—you see? I had hoped...I know...my father is dead, but all of them?" Jon asked explosively. "Part of the changes in my body are because of the death of my father, but I hoped it might mean he was sick, or that others had survived. I watched my father go through the same changes when his father died, but I hoped."

"Oh, Jon, I am so terribly sorry."

With his arms clutched around himself and the ragged remains of his clothes, Jon turned his back to Lu-zan and stumbled away to collapse on the hard ground of the cave. Lu-zan saw, in the early dawn, the wide ridge that ran down Jon's back and the two small projections growing from the base of his skull. Lu-zan didn't know anyone else from the planet Tyrea, so he didn't know whether the changes in Jon were normal or something unique to the ruling family. The traumatic changes were stunning, but the biggest shock was the loss of Jon's hair—his long, flowing mane. If it weren't for his friend's unique eyes, even Matt would not have recognized him. The huge silvery eyes and their blue eyelids were the only feature that seemed the same. *This is my friend, and I'll do all in my power to help him through this,* Lu-zan silently vowed.

"I wish I could give you all the time you need to grieve, but we have to get you out of danger."

"I have to get home."

"You're kidding." Appalled that Jon would even consider such a rash act, Lu-zan whispered, "You can't go home. Didn't you hear me? You're in no condition to go anywhere, especially there."

"Lu-zan, I have no choice…no choice. Look at me. I'm changing. You don't know its meaning, but please take my word."

"You're right. I don't understand, so make me understand. You can start with how you know your father is dead."

Staring dully out at the darkness that surrounded them, Jon swallowed convulsively and rocked back and forth on the rough ground. After a minute, he spoke. Haltingly, then with more urgency, the words poured out.

"My planet…my home…binds my family in service. For centuries, we have served. The planet chooses the eldest in my family, man, woman, or child. The planet chooses the time. Usually, it only happens every 200 or 300 years. But always…it happens." Jon struggled to get the words past his throat to explain. "It chose my father…twelve years ago when my grandfather died. We didn't think it would call me. The one chosen is very long-lived, longer than our normal lifespan of around 150 years. That's why I got to teach off planet. If my father lived, I would not change, but if he died, I would change and become king. My father didn't want me to go, but my mother convinced him. Now…now they possibly are dead, gone, and I'll never, never see them again." The tears were flowing freely. "Now I must go. The planet calls." Jon's hands moved to Lu-zan's arms, holding him as an anchor, his eyes pleading. "Do you understand? I must go."

"I have a lot of questions, but if you need to go home, my questions will have to wait," Lu-zan reassured him. "Somehow, we'll do it. But Jon, if the planet chose you, why are all your relatives dying or missing? Why is the prefect trying to make you a prisoner? What's going on? Is this a hostile takeover? What does Tariq have to do with this? He's running the government right now. Where are the ministers?"

Jon's grief-stricken eyes looked into his. "I don't know. That's part of the reason I have to travel home. There are people I can contact who might know. I have to at least try. People on my planet looked up to my father. I can find help."

"Okay, but you'll need to take a roundabout route to get there. They will watch the spaceports—especially any transports from this planet. We'll work out a plan of our movements. I wish we had time for you to grieve, but we really have to move to keep suspicion low."

CHAPTER 14

The prefect was in a towering rage as he stormed back to the charted ship. His guards tried to stay out of his way. He barricaded himself in his cabin and made plans on how he would tell General Tariq of his failure, and he wondered whether he would live through the experience. Somehow, he had to turn the blame on someone else. The obvious choice was the warden. *Yes,* he thought. *I will place the blame entirely on the warden.*

The guards gathered in their temporary onboard room. They looked at each other nervously. Losing their prey was a new wrinkle in their mission.

The sergeant turned to his adjutant and complained in a low voice. "He will turn on one of us for this." His adjutant cringed and silently pointed to the youngest among them and then turned to the young man and pointed toward the door.

The young soldier shook, and the other guards sent him no sympathetic glances. Each of them wore the scars. Seeing he was not getting any support, Sugan got up and slowly moved to knock on the prefect's door. The guards tried their best to ignore the screams that began to issue from the room. The screams lasted a long time, and the longer they lasted, the more they muttered among themselves. The prefect's long-lasting rage had never been so brutal. Gradually, the sounds died away, and the prefect appeared at his door.

"Get rid of this trash," he ordered, as he stalked away from the room.

The soldiers stared at their comrade. There was blood everywhere, and the tied young soldier lay draped over a wood chair. The sergeant stared in hatred at that chair. He once had been in a similar chair.

The man was barely breathing. Guards gently put him on a cart and took him to the ship's medic. The medic just shook his head and did his best to patch up the results of another one of the prefect's rages. He hoped he could do it again this time.

The sergeant later met with his adjutant privately in his quarters.

"This has got to stop," he complained, as he paced the small space. "He'll kill us all one by one if this keeps up."

"Young Sugen might not make it. The prefect is getting more and more like Tariq," the adjutant dared to complain.

"I know."

"Are we just trading Tariq with someone like the prefect? There is barely any difference between them anymore. I don't think this is worth the money he promised," the adjutant muttered.

The sergeant narrowed his eyes as he studied the other man. "Careful," he admonished. "We definitely do not want that to get back to him."

"I still don't like it. I want to get clear of Tariq, not install another one just like him in his place."

The sergeant sent the adjutant a sly glance. After all, his own agenda called for the prefect to overthrow Tariq. For now, he needed the adjutant to be faithful to him, not the prefect.

A brutish man, the adjutant was big in stature but small in brain power, though he was loyal to the sergeant, who needed him to remain that way. He weighed his options. Was it too soon to reveal his own ambitions and risk that loyalty, or should he simply fan the man's fanatical feelings against the prefect and Tariq? *Yes,* he thought. *I'll talk a little…it is a little safer.*

CHAPTER 15

General Tariq surveyed his domain and liked what he saw, although there were a few loose ends to take care of soon. Returning his attention to the person lying senseless on the floor, he cherished the adrenaline rush he got when he saw the fear bloom on his face. He remembered the first moment he had felt it. It was that last scene with his wife. His young wife of two years had been after him again about having children.

"Tariq, please listen to me," she pleaded with her husband.

"There will be no children in this household. Not now, never. There will be no children, not ours, not our servants. I won't have any rats under my feet," he stormed at her.

"But, when we married, I thought you wanted children."

"No, dear, all I wanted was you and the connections and prestige you could bring me. I have all that, but I find I no longer want or need you." He sneered at her as he moved closer.

She drew back in disgust and the beginnings of fear.

"You are despicable, and I'll file for an annulment," she spat at him and turned toward the door.

He flushed red in anger as he wiped the spittle off his face. He grabbed her savagely by the neck, and at the moment before he hit her, he saw the fear and horror bloom in her eyes. The blow broke her neck, and it confused him to find it saddened him. Not seeing her dead body, but something else. It held him immobile. Murder did not sadden him, but he experienced such a rush of joy at the power of life and death. Surprised, he only wished the feeling had lasted longer. Thoughtfully, he went about covering up his crime. He didn't worry about repercussion—luckily, he already had loyal guards that knew not to cross him. Now, years later, he felt nothing for his dead wife, but he still loved the rush.

This thought brought him back to the man lying on his floor.

"Senator Madden, wake up now. We need to discuss your attitude some more." He nudged the senator roughly with his foot. The senator stirred slightly. "Come now, surely you can see my position?"

The senator slowly, unsteadily, gained his feet. He spat fully into the general's face. The guards stirred and took a step forward, but the general motioned them back and calmly wiped it off. He stared into the senator's eyes and said, "A shame," then calmly broke the senator's neck.

"I'll take that as a no," he said to the body. "Bring in Senator Cipano," he commanded, as he sat back down at his desk.

"Do you want me to remove the body, sir?"

"No. The senators can reunite here." He waved the soldier away.

They escorted the senator in with a soldier holding him up on each side. He noticed in horror the body of Madden on the floor at his feet.

"Senator, so nice of you to join us. I hope your stay has been beneficial for me."

The senator stood rigid and tight-lipped, staring at the general.

"Break his arm," Tariq ordered, and the two soldiers held him while one broke his arm.

When he could stand again, cradling his arm, he remained silent, wondering what else Tariq would do. He looked down at Madden's body, wondering whether he would join him soon.

"Are you going to kill us off one at a time?" His pain-filled voice sounded feeble, even to himself.

"My dear fellow, all this would end if you only agree to back me."

"Why should I back you? For all I know, you have already killed the royal family and imprisoned the senators."

"The royal family is being taken care of; you don't have to worry about them. You need to think about you and your family."

"I sent my family out of harm's way at the first sign of your coup d'état. You'll never find them." The senator stood tall, but Tariq could see the fear start in his eyes. What a sweet sight. He loved seeing the fear bloom and flower in the hearts of his prey. The general pressed a button on his desk and displayed a view of a dungeon cell. The senator stared in disbelief as he saw his wife and oldest daughter holding tight to each other. His other children were not visible to him. He prayed that they, at least, had found refuge.

"What do you want?" he asked.

"I want you to spy for me, that is all. Just report any talk or action against me you see or hear as you go about your duties. Your family will stay in their present accommodations and will remain unharmed if you do what you are told. The alternative is the same fate as Madden. Agreed?"

"Will they then stay unharmed and unmolested by you and your guards?" he asked, looking longingly at his family.

"Of course, my good man. I wouldn't have it any other way."

The senator reluctantly nodded his agreement and was taken away to a doctor to tend his arm.

"Take this trash," Tariq commanded his aide, nudging the dead body with his foot, "and put it in with the senator's lovely wife and child." He thought of his long-ago decision to have no wife and no children. They made such lovely hostages.

"Sir? You have a letter from Minister Wayne," announced one of his soldiers at the door.

Tariq held out his hand for the missive.

After the man had left, Tariq broke the seal and stared at the latest demand for news. When he had left the Southern Military Alliance for the capital city, he knew his plans were much bigger than what the ministers of the Alliance wanted from him. So far, he had ignored the demands for information. This missive was no different, but it did include a threat to travel to see him and take him to task personally.

Calmly, he carried the letter to his desk and set it on fire. Twirling it so the fire spread rapidly, he threw it into the fireplace.

"Come and visit me, dear Minister. I would love to see you," he murmured. "I will even have a welcome surprise, just for you. You can talk with dear Minister Zachari and compare notes. Oh, wait, you can't because Zachari is dead. Maybe you can talk to him in Hell."

And he left the room with a smile on his face that made even his soldiers move back.

One of those soldiers thoughtfully considered what he had overheard as he stood by the door. He quickly left the others as soon as he could and sent a call to Minister Zilri with his interesting news.

CHAPTER 16

When Jon and Alexis flew back in the enclosed air car, the crying of the children over the death of their beloved dog saddened them. Lu-zan tried to distract the children by telling them stories of his homeland.

Jon had a bad time traveling through the forest and waiting to climb into the container. He was weaker than he thought. The rest of the party had struggled to get him and Phillip back to the camp using the anti-gravity disc. He didn't fit into the container because of his height, but he was so tired he actually fell asleep next to Phillip on the floor of the air car. Mari and the kids asked a lot of questions that Lu-zan and Alexis tried to answer. The kids were especially fascinated by Jon. Alexis found peace watching him sleep and listening to the banter from the group in the air car.

Mari, Phillip, and the kids had made their farewell a moment to remember by giving their guests cookies for their trip off planet. Lu-zan delighted in receiving lots of his favorite fruits. Alexis checked Phillip one last time before they left.

"Thank you for all your help," Jon said to the family. "Maybe one day I can explain to you what this means to me. I will never forget your bravery and kindness for as long as I live."

Alexis drew Phillip aside and gave him a huge hug. Turning to the rest of the family, she thanked each gravely and wished them to be safe after they left.

Jon and Alexis ended up needing to squeeze themselves into the container after all. Lu-zan traveled back to the spaceport with the container in tow, but no one questioned him about it or what it contained. The surrounding people assumed the container had provisions from that trip and not a very uncomfortable Jon and Alexis.

When Lu-zan and the contained got back into their quarters, he opened the container to let a relieved Jon and Alexis climb out. Jon stretched his back and moaned. "I think you enjoyed that," he accused Lu-zan with a wry grin. Lu-zan offered a back rub to Alexis but laughed when Jon glared at him. Lu-zan offered one of his precious fruits in appeasement. He graciously gave way to Jon with a shake of his hand in Alexis' direction. Jon smiled and bit into the fruit.

Lu-zan was very grateful they had assigned him a large space on board the ship. They would need it with two extra people. There were several problems that needed to be addressed as soon as possible.

"Could you come to my quarters as promptly as you can? And could you bring the ship's doctor, too? Thank you," Lu-zan requested of the ship's captain.

"Why are you asking for another doctor? I can examine Jon," Alexis said, as she tried to hold on to her temper.

He gently told her, "We don't need another doctor for Jon. We need the ship's doctor in order to ration food, oxygen, and other consumables, which are finite on board a ship. We now have two extra people on board that will cause adjustments. No one is questioning your expertise, Doctor. We are all very impressed with your skill in dealing with this one." He gestured to Jon.

"Oh, I'm sorry for assuming otherwise," Alexis answered levelly.

"No need to apologize. You are just not used to thinking in terms of payloads." He smiled, and she smiled back.

The prized fruits were being carefully unwrapped by Lu-zan. Mari had sent enough for the entire crew, and so Lu-zan was being especially careful. He handed one each to Jon and Alexis and reserved one for himself, but he laid the rest in a container to give to the crew. He laughed when he saw the look on Jon's face as he bit into his fruit. Alexis blissfully said, "If I had known that Mari could make ambrosia, I would have made it a point to meet her earlier. I think Phillip has been holding out on me. What a wonderful treat."

Jon looked at Lu-zan when a knock sounded at the door. He and Alexis retreated to the bedrooms section of the quarters to conceal themselves until Lu-zan signaled that it was okay. Jon knew both of the visitors, so he waited for Lu-zan to signal him an okay to emerge. They only appeared when the okay came, and the doctors made introductions. Lu-zan explained about Jon and the prefect.

"Jon, that is terrible. Of course we will help," interjected the captain.

"Captain, what Jon went through has resulted in physical changes, as you can see. I want to document them. Then we will need to disguise him so he can have freedom of movement."

"I'll need an extensive disguise," Jon said lightly.

"In part, that is why I wanted to meet with you in my quarters. Dr. Michaels has done a remarkable job with the injuries Jon suffered from the crash, but mostly she has been working without information on Tyrean physiology. I thought Dr. Aorangi and Dr. Michaels could well use our time by asking Jon to submit to a more detailed examination to set a baseline to help in his care. Also, is there any way to change his eye color and eyelid dye?"

"Of course. With Dr. Michaels' help, we can use the ship's extensive medical lab and database to help," Dr. Aorangi replied. "I've wanted to examine Jon for years—medically, of course." Her eyes twinkled as Jon blushed.

"He will need a few sets of clothing also; the last set didn't survive the crash, so Phillip donated what he is wearing," Lu-zan said, eyeing the ill-fitting ones covering Jon.

"Captain, I also wanted to plan a stop to get supplies." The captain and Lu-zan sat down to go over star maps, and Jon went with the two doctors, who discussed tests that they should run.

Later, Lu-zan took advantage of the time to work with Jon and Alexis on relaxation techniques. Jon was already familiar with them, so Lu-zan spent most of the time working with Alexis, who, though she listened to what Lu-zan was saying, also kept a close eye on Jon as he went through his routine. Lu-zan also monitored Jon, noting that he was tiring.

"Hey, slow up a little," Alexis protested. "I'm new to all this."

"You're right. We should take a break," Lu-zan said in agreement.

Jon was happy to take a break. It dismayed him to discover how tired and sore he was. He had thought the cocoon had healed him completely.

Jon retired to his bedroom, where he fell into a deep, healing sleep. This put Alexis at ease as it assuaged her that he was finally able to fully relax. Sleep had already proven extraordinarily good for Jon, but this was the first time he could really stretch out to his full height.

They could tell the ship was getting ready to arrive at their next destination, the moon colony of Obadiah, which orbited a protected planet in the yellow dwarf star system of X-Arlo. The X also appeared in front of the particular planet in the system that was protected. Here, the planetary name was X-Upid. Scientists routinely fought for a chance to study everything about the minor planet, from the smallest ameba to the largest living organism. The uniqueness of the planet stemmed from the fact that it had no native species and what existed there now had somehow travelled from somewhere else. But how and when were the questions. Scientists had been scrambling to answer the question of panspermia on this unique world. So, an exchange had developed on the only moon where ships could bring supplies for free docking privileges, which resulted in a sizable marketplace.

Jon, dressed in his new clothes, stood with Alexis watching the action at the docking facility. He was amazed at some items used to gain docking space. He spied Souse ale from the planet Geneve and air car parts from planet Ford. The entire group did some shopping at the market in the docking dome.

Jon and Alexis had a great time expanding their wardrobe—especially Jon, who clowned around trying on wigs and hats.

"What do you think of this one?" he asked, modeling a wig of blue hair long enough to hang down his back to his waist. "Too much?"

"I like it. We could braid it sometimes." She hid her smile as she studied the wig. "It might be a little long."

He finally settled on two wigs: one which covered the growths and was a color that matched his silver eyes, and a second one to pair with contacts to change his eye color. Also, he purchased skin cream to tint his skin. Unfortunately, he couldn't do anything about his height. Alexis relied on changing her hair color and small lifts in her shoes to change her height. She also had her eyelids temporarily dyed blue to match Jon's.

"Will this be enough to fool anyone looking for us?" Alexis asked, tugging on her larger dress.

"People look at surface features to recognize someone. You don't need a lot of changes. Your height alone will mark you as being from off world. I have the same problem. It's nice to have some new clothes. I really enjoyed getting something new to wear."

"What's the next stop? Another planet or your home world?"

"Well, Matt promised Lu-zan that he would reserve hotel rooms when we get to Clete—that's the nearest planet to my home world. You will love it. It has a neat collection of natural wildlife; it just didn't develop any higher species. Human settlement there started about five hundred years ago and has been going strong ever since. It's an agricultural planet and is really our breadbasket in the sky. It's a beautiful world with a lot of natural wonders."

"It sounds lovely. Maybe we should just stay there," she murmured.

"I wish we could, but I need to get home. My father has a friend who is a senator. I should go to him first and find out what the situation is and see if he can help us."

"Is he reliable? Are you sure of his loyalties? It has been a long while. People do change."

"Well, that's true, but I have little choice. He is one official high enough in the government that I remember. We'll travel to his home and watch first in case things have changed. Then maybe we can get to talk to him."

"Okay, Jon, we'll do that, but first I have something I need to say. We've known each other for only a brief time. I want nothing to happen to you, because I like you, but also, I don't want to be left alone on this planet. I know Lu-zan is coming down to your planet later, but I admit, I'm scared for us both."

He realized Alexis was becoming very important to him. She had given up everything to help him, and he was grateful for all she had done, but he realized his feelings were becoming deeper than that now. He wanted to be with her and protect her from all danger. Unfortunately, she was in more danger because she was with him. Maybe he could remedy that and get her somewhere safe, away from him. It amazed him that she felt the same. At least, he hoped she felt the same.

"When we get to Tyrea, maybe you should stay somewhere you'll be sheltered while I go alone to the senator's residence," he whispered. Surprise took him when she reared back from him in anger.

"You are not going anywhere without me. You still need me to help you heal," she said, fire in her eyes. "And yes, I'm scared, but I am not a coward."

"I just want you to be safe," he said, looking deep into her eyes. "You are NOT a coward for being scared. No coward would rescue me from a prison or travel all over with me. I think you are one of the strongest and bravest women I know."

It took a long time to sleep. Grief and worry were playing havoc with his mind—replaying the attack, the confinement on the prefect's ship and the cruelty of his guards, the crash on the prison planet, and the acknowledgement of his father's death. After all the pain and worry, he couldn't believe he had found someone so courageous. His eyes closed with thoughts of Alexis in all her moods. When sleep came, he was smiling.

Later, after dusk, Jon became aware that something was wrong. He lay still and listened, wondering what could have woken him up. A faint noise sounded from the empty bedroom next to his room. He looked at the clock and realized that they had only been asleep for a couple of hours. He got up and crept to his bedroom door, looking for anything he could use as a weapon. Not seeing anything he could use, he moved to the door to Alexis' room and whispered her name.

She awoke instantly, but when she saw Jon, she realized that he was signaling for her to be quiet. He pointed to the window, and they moved silently toward it. There was a ledge outside, so they began to move cautiously out onto it.

"Jon?" Matt said quietly from behind him. They froze and turned to see Matt grinning at them. "Want to come back?" he asked. His eyes danced mischievously as he eyed Jon and Alexis in their nightwear.

The two of them inched back to the window. Matt helped them both back into the room. As soon as they were inside, Jon rounded on Matt.

"When did you get here? What are you doing here?" he yelled. "Why tiptoe around the other room? Alexis could have fallen to her death." He rubbed his hands over his bare head and down over his face.

Matt grinned. "We just didn't want to wake you."

"We?" Alexis asked him, as she grabbed a robe.

Lu-zan peeked around the doorway between the two rooms. "I sincerely apologize, my friends."

"We came up with an alternate plan to get you to Tyrea. We found a small supply shuttle going to the surface from the space station. Lu-zan and I are to stop there as part of a standard tour of potential training sites. We can get you to the space station and then onto the shuttle. The problem is the shuttle is going to the southern spaceport. You and Alexis will have to travel overland to the capital alone, but your disguises should be foolproof."

"How soon can we go?" Jon asked, already turning to grab their packs.

"Jon, first you need to rest. That's why Lu-zan and I were trying to be quiet and not wake you. The transport leaves tomorrow at 10:43 a.m., and you will need to be at the port by 9:00 a.m. local time, which gives you time to sleep and eat."

"Let's get some sleep before the next leg of the trip tomorrow," Alexis suggested, as she moved away. "Our ship leaves at 10:32 a.m., and we have to be at the spaceport by 9:00 a.m. That only lets us have six hours of sleep."

Lu-zan came forward. "My son, you must do this. It is the most secure way to get to the planet's surface."

Jon reluctantly agreed. "Next time, don't scare us like that."

"Hopefully, there won't be a next time."

CHAPTER 17

For all of his blustering, the prefect was shaking as he walked to General Tariq's office. His failure to deliver Jon was a complete disaster, but if nothing else, he was a survivor so far. He knocked on the door and waited for permission to enter. At least his troops would not witness his humiliation. They knew, and it had the bigger benefit that they viewed him as one of them.

General Tariq was sitting at his desk, pulling his hand up and down the staff he loved to use on people. The prefect watched him stroking that staff, knowing the enjoyment the general got when he applied it to someone's back or legs. *It's ironic,* thought the prefect, *that we share the same enjoyment.*

"Would you care to explain why you have returned without the cargo I asked you to pick up?"

The prefect watched as the general continued to stroke the staff up and down. He could feel his body yearning for it. He hated that part of himself, but the pleasure was so intense.

"Everything went as clockwork when we initially picked up the prince, but the ship developed a problem. We were lucky that it crashed on a prison planet. Several of us got injured, including him. I had to have him treated. The warden was not very cooperative. The prince somehow escaped, either on his own or maybe he had help."

"Take off your coat," demanded the general.

Trembling with fear, the prefect removed his coat and risked a quick glance as the general stopped stroking the staff. The prefect rushed on with his explanation.

"The warden refused to search for the prince, so I had to do that myself. I also had to search the grounds of the prison, and I tried to search outside the grounds, but the warden got the air patrol to stop the search. They even killed a couple of my men. It's amazing I escaped with my life. I thought he would try to come home."

"Strip all the way," demanded the general, ignoring all the prefect's excuses. Now he was shaking all over. Already he could feel the excitement and dread building in his body. "Take your clothes to the other room," the general told him.

"Hmm, that is an interesting idea. If he came home, where would he go for help? Senator Aeneas' name comes to mind, since he was an old friend of the family. I have been removing ministers whom I don't like for some time now. Yes, he would probably go to the senator for help. Walk to the wall and turn around," the general continued, as he calmly fastened the restraints to the prefect's ankles and wrists. He also secured a belt around the prefect's waist. Now he was really shaking.

"I can pick the senator up, sir," he pleaded, eager to make up for his mistake.

"You will not be in any shape to do that. We will be busy for a while, you and I." The general closed the soundproof door.

The prefect stood staring at the gray wall across the room, waiting for that first lash to fall. He hated the anticipation he felt, and he loved it also, but this time, he knew it was going to be especially bad. That was one thing he didn't understand: why he loved the lashings so much and hated the one giving it. *One of these times, I am going to break that cane.* He sighed, knowing he never would. He closed his eyes and told himself it could have been worse. Yes, it could have been much worse. He could be dead and miss the pleasure to come.

"Shall we start?" asked Tariq.

CHAPTER 18

Tariq summoned Senator Aeneas to an audience. Aeneas was not a fan of Tariq. They had served together on the Planetary Board, but Aeneas couldn't stand or trust him. Oh, he was nice enough, but Aeneas felt uneasy around him. He feared what he could want with him, especially since so many people had gone missing. The senator suspected the general might have something to do with it. Now he was about to see the man.

He turned to the guards that the general had sent to escort him. "I need my coat," he said, hurrying down the hall. He was frantic to get to the kitchen and his daughter.

"Anya, come here, dear," he whispered, so the guards would not hear. "Do you know where my blue coat is?" he asked in a louder voice, signaling to Anya to keep quiet by putting his finger across his lips.

Looking at him questioningly, she walked over to him. He leaned down and whispered in her ear. "I'm afraid General Tariq has sent his guards to take me to an audience with him. I'm wondering if I'll return. Some senators are missing, and I am wondering if he is responsible."

Anya looked alarmed.

"Pack some clothes and go to your cousin Yancey's house. I'll come to you as soon as I can. I love you. Hurry now." He kissed her forehead and hurried out to the hall closet.

"Ah, here it is."

The guards bundled the senator into the air car waiting out front. Anya hurried to a window to see him leave, then she rushed to carry out his wishes.

The senator watched the city speed by as the air car rose toward the palace and wondered whether he would live to see it again. His late wife had loved flowers in gold and blue hues and had planted them all over the estate that he had built for their family. The massive trees framed the expanse of the house and acreage beautifully. Now he doubted whether he would see them or his family ever again.

People below went about their normal lives, completely oblivious to how deeply their government had sunk. He would like to live to be part of the solution and end the madness of General Tariq. He remembered when Tariq had first appeared at the assembly as the representative from the Northern Military Alliance, which had always been more extremely militant and considered radical. The Northern Alliance was on the next largest island, separated from the capital, which was on the largest island on the planet. But something was happening here in the Eastern Alliance capital. Tariq was now taking control because some very important people had gone missing. Aeneas was sure that Tariq was making a grab for power, and it must stop, but no one was sure how.

The palace came into view, and he could feel his body tense. *Did anyone else besides Anya know about this meeting? If he disappeared or was killed, would anyone even know?* he wondered. He didn't have answers for any of his whirling questions.

The palace gates flashed by as the air car prepared to land. They ushered the senator out of the car and through a side door. He looked around, noticing that in the cleared halls, no one would see him. That answered one of his questions, and he felt it didn't bode well for his future. Soon they came to the general's office, where they pushed the senator into a room, the guards taking up posts outside the door.

Aeneas straightened his clothes and looked around the room. Silently, he noticed other doors, placement of the windows—which he checked to see whether they were unlocked—and he especially looked for any type of surveillance equipment. He then quietly took a seat and waited and waited and waited. Hours later, General Tariq and the prefect finally came in the door.

Okay, point taken, thought the senator. *I'm here at your leisure.* He noticed the prefect seemed to limp a little as he passed him. The senator took a quick look at the prefect's face, catching a grimace as the man moved. *So, Tariq is also in control of the prefect. Interesting,* thought Aeneas.

"Here you are," Tariq said in a pleasant tone.

No title, another bad sign, thought the senator.

"I think you know the prefect."

"What do you want, Tariq?" He purposefully ignored the prefect. "I have work, if you don't."

"Oh, you will do what I tell you."

"What do you mean?" said the senator. Tariq was too sure of himself. What did he have up his sleeve? He glanced at the prefect, but no help came from him. The prefect looked ill, as if he were in pain. The senator wondered what hold Tariq had on the prefect to force him to comply. He, himself, had taken precautions because of the unrest. All the household staff had the week off. He had wanted them safe with their families. *I hope Anya got out of the house in time,* he prayed, *to get to her cousin's home outside the city limits.*

Where are the king and queen? he wondered. Other ministers were missing. He didn't know whether they had left at the beginning of the troubles or if Tariq had them in cells. He hoped the growing list of names did not include his—that he, too, would find himself soon inhabiting one of those cells.

"What I mean, Senator, is I need you to do me a favor. Just a little favor, among friends. A matter has come up, and you will be at the center."

"What is it?"

"Well, I'm expecting a representative of the royal family, and I think they will ask you to bring them to the palace. I just need you to deliver him or her to me."

"Whomever it is doesn't need me to take him or her to the palace. They are welcome here. They live here after all."

"You don't understand me. Let me make myself clearer. I require you to lead him or them to ME. I do not wish anyone to know they are here."

"What do you plan to do?" The senator rose out of his chair, and arms appeared from behind him, pushing him back down. He twisted to see who was there. Guards and the prefect had moved behind him. His heart leaped into his throat. Next, Tariq would begin his threats. He wondered what Tariq could come up with to threaten him. His wife had been dead for many years, and he had sent his daughter away. He had lived a long life with few regrets.

"Why do you think I'll help you?"

"Let me show you." He signaled to one of his soldiers.

Senator Aeneas looked around, fear gripping his throat. "Oh no," he whispered in despair.

"Oh yes, my dear Senator. I have your beautiful daughter. I don't want to harm her, and I won't if you do what I tell you to do. Understand now?"

Aeneas looked at the terrified, but still defiant, face of his child. He knew he would do anything to keep her alive, including betraying the royal family. God forgive him, but he had to keep her safe.

Anya looked at her father and saw the defeat in his eyes. "Don't do it, Father. He'll kill us anyway." She didn't want him bartering with Tariq for her freedom, but she could see the fear and defeat in her father's face.

He couldn't take the chance. "Do you promise not to harm her?"

"I am a man of compassion. Ask the prefect, who failed at the small errand I gave him to do, and he is still alive. Isn't that right, Prefect?"

"You are very compassionate, General." The prefect glanced uneasily at the general as he spoke.

"Take her away." Tariq waved the guard and prisoner away. Turning to the senator, he saw the defeated look on his face and could smell the fear.

Taking a deep breath, the senator slowly nodded his head. Looking up at Tariq, he pleaded and promised in the same sentence, "You harm her, I WILL make you pay."

"Of course, my dear Senator, I don't want to hurt a single hair on her head. Take him and his daughter back home. A guard will watch at all times, so don't run or send your daughter to shelter. You will be sorry. Goodbye, Senator."

The guards pushed him into an air car quicker than when he had arrived. He protested that his daughter was not with him. He worried that Tariq had lied, and he wouldn't return Anya to him. The guards said nothing. He could have been a piece of meat that they were delivering. He wanted to kick or beat someone, preferably Tariq, or one of his guards. They arrived back at his home without his even being aware of the trip. His thoughts went round and round, worrying how he could betray his close friends and how could he not, because of Anya. He felt his upset stomach churn, and he hoped he wouldn't embarrass himself. Better yet, maybe he could throw up on the guards' boots.

When he opened his front door, it shocked him to find he was being squeezed to death. Looking down, he realized the person doing the squeezing was his beloved daughter. He put his arms around her and squeezed her right back. The guard quietly closed the door and stood waiting. The senator looked at him and took a step toward him, his hands clenched. Anya cried out and put herself between them.

"Father, Father, no, you don't understand," Anya cried, as she faced her father.

"What...what don't I understand?" he demanded, as he continued to glare at the guard.

Anya looked sheepish. The guard had the grace to look at his boots. Visibly gathering her courage, Anya took the man's hand and brought him closer.

"Father, Willem is here to watch us, but he is also my special friend. He has been very helpful to me but also to the queen."

"Sir, I am no true soldier for General Tariq. He is truly an evil man. I have been part of his guard unit for the last six months. He has ordered some ministers imprisoned, intimidated, and murdered. Also, I found the queen trying to walk down a hallway. She was badly injured and was trying to find shelter. I got her to a hideout. The general has ordered the guards to find her. I hope she is disguised enough till I can get her some additional help. I want to do more. What else can I do?"

The senator eyed him and tried to gauge the truth or whether he could take a chance and believe him. He looked at his daughter's hopeful face and sighed.

"Do you know what Tariq is doing? Do you know what Tariq threatened?" he demanded to know, as he glared at Willem.

"He hurt the queen. I haven't been privy to everything, but I know enough that I had to step in today. Sir, I heard part of what he asked you to do. You can't do it, sir. I feel Prince Jon is the key to our salvation."

The senator was not willing to meet the eyes of his daughter. "I can't take a chance with Anya's life. I'm sorry I am not so brave when it comes to your safety." His eyes pleaded that she understand. "I don't know what to answer. With you here, I can at least try to warn whoever is coming from the royal family."

"Father, the fight has come to us. We all have to do what we can. That includes me and Willem. We are young, but we still have to do our part." Anya tried to make him understand. "Mother would have insisted she fight with you. Besides, Prince Jon might have a plan."

"Sir, maybe we can plan something to help destroy the general's plans. Meanwhile, I can try to discover what happened to the rest of the royal family. I hope the hideout for the queen is a shrouded enough place, but no one knows where the others are."

"Wait, do you mean, except for Jon and the queen, the rest are all missing?" The senator could feel his panic rising. The king was an intrinsic part of the power grid for the planet. He didn't understand how, but it always called on the royal family to manage the power of the core. When he became a senator, he was told about their special connection to the planet. This knowledge was privileged information and not something he could share.

"Let me think for a moment." He walked away from the young couple. *If Tariq was making a power grab, he would need to get rid of all the royal family and get control of the senators and ministers. They could have gone into hiding, or Tariq could have them in dungeons, or the third option, they could be dead. Is this a power grab by the Northern Alliance, or is Tariq making a play for power on his own? Well, we will deal with one problem at a time. Tariq had demanded that he bring the royal family member that is coming to him.*

He knew all the royal family members—the king, queen, three sons, and one daughter. They were his friends. Jon, the eldest son, was off planet working as a survival guide or something, so it must be Jon who was coming.

"Willem, can you investigate what happened to the royal family? Or, at least, check the dungeons for them? I don't know when this royal person will show up."

Willem nodded. "But, sir, I'm supposed to stay here and watch you and Anya."

"Will anyone relieve you, or do you need to check-in somehow?"

"I have to check in every four hours, and you and Anya have to be seen on-screen. I still need to check for listening devices in the other rooms. I already checked this room and closed the doors on this floor. They shouldn't be able to hear us talking."

"Okay, we will check in regularly and work on a plan. In the meantime, the household staff will be back next week, and maybe we can use their help without endangering them. Can you make an off-planet call without getting caught?"

"Yes, sir. I have off-planet access on my private phone."

"Okay, let's do this. Call the Intergalactic Police and report the royal family as missing. That should start a check on them. I'm surprised Tariq hasn't cut your access, but I don't think he wants to stir up the public yet. Since he has instigated more patrols and tighter restrictions on gatherings, the public is already on edge. At least, that's a first step. We'll figure out the rest as we go along." The senator gripped Willem's shoulder and gave his daughter a hug.

CHAPTER 19

The palace was in an uproar. The king and queen were missing, the children were missing, Prince Jon was off planet, and the servants were whispering in the hallways. Rumors were flying faster than an intergalactic ship. Gregory and his wife, Suri, worried. They loved their monarch, his wife and family, but they also loved their son. They worried about the security of their king and queen. Especially, they worried about their son, who had recently been assigned as a guard for General Tariq. Assignment as a guard was a significant promotion since the general was an important personage, but there was one problem. They didn't like him; he had the reputation of a braggart and a cheat. He used to go into town and gamble significant amounts of his wealth. Lately, the gossips said that he was gambling a lot, but it wasn't his money. His young wife had died suddenly, and he had mourned in public, but Suri had seen his smirk when he didn't think anyone was looking. He was rude to the staff, treated his guards worse, and was sneaky. Neither Gregory nor Suri trusted him to treat their son well. Now, the general's puppet was back. The prefect was just a hanger-on of the general. Everyone knew that. No one trusted him either.

Suri bustled around the apartment, wanting to keep busy so she couldn't think. She worried about what the general and the prefect had in store, and now her son was among that group of vipers. Gregory watched her and worried for them both. The apartment was already clean, but he said nothing. He knew his wife and agreed with her method of dealing with stress and worry.

"Has anyone said they have seen any of the royal family?"

Suri shook her head. "No one is allowed to clean the royal apartments." She moved the pillows around the chairs for the fourth time in the last five minutes.

He got up and gave her shoulder a pat. "I think I'll go down to the stables. Maybe I can get some more information." He descended the stairs. Well-liked and popular, he greeted staff on his way. Most of the staff knew him, and many people visited him and his horses. Gregory was very proud of his horses, especially since he had talked the king into importing them from Earth. People couldn't help but love horses. They were just so beautiful. The royal family loved them, and various personages also had imported horses of their own to keep in the royal stables.

When he got to the stables, it amazed him to find several grooms working. It was late. He soon found out why so many were there. Draven was telling stories again. Grooms loved to listen to his stories about the building of the palace and the stables. The buildings were thousands of years old. Gregory didn't know whether all the stories were true, but Draven was a great history buff and could have done some research. He had the talent to weave a story out of the smallest fact.

Gregory stood for a while and listened, and then he went into the office he kept there. He worked on his ledgers and enjoyed the sweet smell of the hay and the monotone of voices from the stalls. A change in the tone of the voices alerted him when an unfamiliar voice joined them. He went to the door of his office. He saw that the unknown voice belonged to a guard from General Tariq's staff.

His well-trained grooms wouldn't do anything that the guard would take offense at, but he noted the cool, bordering on chilly, reception the guard received.

"Hey you," the guard said, pointing to one groom. "My horse needs to be rubbed down and fed," he demanded, snapping his fingers.

"Yes, sir," answered one of the oldest grooms, who took the sweaty and tired horse's reins. The groom led the horse down the aisle toward a stall. The guard watched them, then turned his back and stalked away.

The grooms crowded around the older groom, throwing out suggestions of things he could do to the horse in retaliation. The old groom listened and said, "I think this here horse deserves extra grain. Look at what he has to put up with day after day." He murmured to the animal and gave him a good rubdown and a couple of cups of extra grain.

"Why do that? That guard will just expect it from now on," complained one groom.

"Our job is to take care of these animals, and we do that to the best of our ability. I won't do less than that just because someone is mean. Besides, it ain't this animal's fault his master is a jackass."

Gregory smiled and nodded his head. He stayed and listened for a while more and left, saying nothing. The atmosphere in the stables eased, and the group soon split up. Gregory knew he wouldn't learn any new information that night.

Gregory returned to his desk and continued to work for a while more, but he wanted to get back to Suri. Needing to be held, they could comfort each other in these dangerous times. He hoped his son did not act anything like the boorish soldier who had visited his stables. He thought his son wouldn't dare behave that way, because everyone knew him, and Willem knew his parents would find out if that were the case. Gregory knew he wouldn't have to do a thing. His Suri would take care of Willem. The thought made him smile.

CHAPTER 20

The space station floated in black space, looking serene with its transparent dome. The Intergalactic Police transport bumped the docking link. As the link closed and air hissed in, the door telescoped open. They marched down the ramp to meet the head of the IP training delegation.

After the greetings were over, Matt indicated the chests being carried down the ramp.

"I have a favor to ask. Can you put those on the transport to the planet? I have someone meeting them at the spaceport. Here are the clearance papers and certificates." He handed over the forged documents.

"I would appreciate gentle treatment for this one chest in particular. It contains delicate equipment," supplied Lu-zan.

"Of course, sir." Turning, the officer ordered a soldier to put a "DELICATE" sticker on that chest. Turning back, he added, "Right this way, sir. I have ideas about how to use the space station as a training tool."

"Excellent. I hope we can come up with some challenging exercises."

While they toured the space station, the crew carried the chests to the transport, a standard two deck carrier with a large cargo hold.

It carried a crew of ten, which included a pilot, co-pilot, navigator, cargo manager, and six cargo crew members. Activity was brisk, and they handled the two chests a little roughly since the manager wasn't there to oversee the loading of the cargo hold. They packed the chests with other boxes on top and put them on a rack with telescoping straps that would hold them securely in place. The crew stayed in the pressurized hold with the cargo, which was lucky for Jon and Alexis. A little while later, the crew finished up and got into their restraints for take-off. Then they waited.

Jon and Alexis could hear the crew talking, mostly complaining about conditions on the planet, company policies changing, and about their pay. They talked about their families being upset with all the new soldiers on the streets and the fear that seemed to lie beneath the surface. Jon strained to hear any information about what was happening.

The workers had little to do until the transport put down on the surface. Then they were busy. The yard became crowded with boxes and crates. It looked like controlled chaos, with machines moving briskly up and down aisles. It took most of the afternoon to unload everything. Then the crew took time off for dinner, and the area became silent. Jon and Alexis listened for a few minutes to ensure no one was around. They checked the mechanism in their container to ensure it worked, hoping they had not damaged it in the loading and unloading process. Jon activated the mechanism, and the side of the chest slid open. Both them and their backpacks rolled out at the same time. Laughing quietly, they untangled themselves and crept around the corner and out of the yard.

The yard was silent for a few more minutes until the workers returned. The forklifts started up and moved down the various aisles. One worker on a forklift had just passed an aisle when she noticed something odd about one crate. She stopped and changed directions to check. When she got close, she noticed the number on the crate and that it was empty. She called the main office to report the opened crate. Her duty done, she reversed directions to go back to her errand. Later, an officer hurried over to the chest. Checking the manifest, he saw there were two crates listed. He hurried to check the second crate, only to find it, too, was open and empty.

Dammit, the Director of Pyrotechnics sent these crates according to this cargo invoice. I wonder if any of the locals took them for a bit of fun. Anyway, I need to get in touch with the director's office and let him know about his missing fireworks. Why he would want fireworks on this planet is beyond me, thought the officer.

CHAPTER 21

Willem kept checking over his shoulder as he hurried down the street. He didn't see anyone behind him, but everyone was so edgy that he couldn't help looking. General Tariq was insane, and when the time came, he hoped to be the one to kill him. Meanwhile, it was more important to keep his mind on his mission. Everyone he loved was in danger.

He entered the palace through the secret passage he had found when he was a child. He didn't know how many others might know of it, but in all the years he'd used it, he had seen no one else near it. Its simplicity had served him well. His mission was to listen and try to find out more about the royal family. He had made his way carefully to the royal suite. No one seemed to be around. He searched the king and queen's suite but learned nothing. It tempted him to check on the queen, but he feared a guard walking in and catching them in the bolt-hole. The royal family had always lived simply within the palace, which had been built long ago in appreciation for them and the planet that had given so much through the centuries. It was immaculate, like it had just been cleaned. In the daughter's room, he found clothes tossed about and some mess, but nothing suspicious. He moved on to the younger brothers' area. There was a different story told in these rooms, where blood was on the walls and floor. The overturned and broken furniture proved a fight had taken place here.

Looking into every cabinet and wardrobe, Willem hoped there was a secret passage somewhere, so some of the royal family could have escaped. He saw no evidence of one, but if it were cleverly hidden, he might not see it. He tapped on all the walls, furniture, and wardrobe, looking for any hidden latches, pushing and pulling every sconce on the walls. Retracing his steps, he went back into every suite. He hoped he had missed none. The king and queen's set of rooms were a small maze. They had added to it and remodeled many times throughout the centuries.

"What are you doing here?" came a rough voice.

Startled, Willem turned to see a guard just coming into the room.

"General Tariq wanted these rooms searched, sir!" he announced, as he snapped a salute.

"I have searched these other rooms," the soldier lied, "but carry on. It wouldn't hurt to be checked twice." He left Willem to finish the job. "I'll just tell the general," he said, knowing he would take full credit for the job.

Willem continued to look around, looking at areas he knew were not passageways, in case the soldier came back.

A little later, Willem found it in the king and queen's suite. It was a chest of drawers that swung out to reveal a hidden passageway behind it. That led to a set of descending stairs. Willem quietly entered the dark passageway and closed the chest of drawers behind him. Carefully, he went down two flights of stairs until he came to two branching passageways going in different directions. He looked at the floor and saw footprints leading down the dust-covered steps. He knew that over the centuries, the passageway had not been often used because a fine layer of dust had accumulated. Whoever had come down had left a clear set of footprints to follow as he descended the stairs.

Taking off his inner shirt, he swept across the floor of the passage so no prints would show, swirling the dust and masking any potential trail. Backtracking, he did the same in the opposite passageway. He followed the footprints until he came to another stairway. Because the footprints did not continue, he stepped around the opening and continued down the passageway for about another ten yards. He then went to the stairway and started down. Three more times he swept away the footprints.

He knew the level for housing of the head of household staff. His parents lived on this level. He noticed the footprints spaced a little closer, as if the person were unsure or looking for something. He slowed down in order to watch the footsteps more carefully. Some walls were thinner in places, and he could hear sounds. He started looking for peepholes and soon located one. He looked through it and saw a corridor with doors leading to rooms that seemed uninhabited. A light was on, but no sound or movements showed. He closed the peephole and continued down the passageway, still following the footprints.

He soon heard a muffled sound ahead. It was a brief scuff that stopped him immediately. He inched forward and realized the sound had come from around a bend in the passageway. He stood still and listened. *Was that a soft sob?* he wondered. Unsure of what he had heard, he moved closer and peered around the corner. What he saw made him gasp. The involuntary sound made the young girl he saw scuttle back in fear.

He immediately put his hands up to show her he didn't have a weapon. "Hello, my name is Willem," he quietly said to allay her fear. She kept staring at his uniform and trembling. "It's okay, honest. I'm one of the good guys," he said, when he realized he had forgotten he had on his uniform. She didn't look like she believed him.

He had seen the princess many times, but only at a distance. She was around fifteen years old, a lively teenager, and Willem knew she loved chocolate-covered cherries. His mother was the head upstairs maid in the palace, and all the household staff knew the royal family. All of them loved the princess. This dirty, frightened girl hardly looked like the polished, sheltered princess, but he would recognize her anywhere. Somehow, he had to convince her to trust him.

"Princess Leni, I am the son of Gregory and Suri Young, the head groom and head upstairs maid here at the palace. They assigned me to General Tariq's guard, and that's why I'm wearing his uniform. Please, don't be afraid. I'm trying to find your family. Do you know if any other escaped?"

"Why do you want to know? So you can tell General Tariq?" she asked tearfully, but bravely. "You could be one of them, or you could turn me over to one of them. Why should I trust you?"

"Yes, I could, but I won't. I could take you to meet my parents, but I think you don't know them very well. You would have seen them, so that wouldn't prove anything. During my childhood, I played with Prince Jon, and we ran around the lower floors of the palace, so I know my way around. I think you want out of the palace. I know a way. It's another secret passage."

She watched him for a long time.

"Princess Leni, I must get back to my charge, and it might be a good thing for you to come with me. I'm supposed to be watching Senator Aeneas and his daughter. General Tariq wants him to betray a member of your family who is coming here. I'm not sure who it is, but I think it's probably your brother, Jon. I have to report soon. We have a plan, and I think you may be safer with the senator. Please, will you come?"

"Okay," she said simply, surprising him.

"Okay?" he asked, stunned. "Okay, this way then." He turned down the passageway, dragging his shirt behind him. She gave him a strange look until he explained. She looked surprised and chagrined that she hadn't noticed her footprints. He led her down two more floors until they reached the lowest levels. The passageway had deteriorated as they descended. The stone was still solid, but it had a lot of dust and mold. It made sneezing a very real hazard. He hoped neither of them gave into the urge to sneeze because someone might hear it through the walls. Accumulated dust gave evidence that no one had used the stairs in a long time, and he hadn't used them in about ten years. Hopefully, there wouldn't be any surprises.

Princess Leni tried not to show her unease over the mold-covered walls and the squeaks of little creatures as they hid from the light. Willem's whispered encouragement helped, and she didn't want him to know how afraid she really was. They continued back down the passageway until they came upon a heavy, iron-bound door.

"This leads to another tunnel, but I want to warn you, it's rougher than this one. Just follow my lead, and we'll get through all right. Ready?"

She nodded in reply.

The first thing she noticed when he opened the door was odor. It smelled like dirt, not dust. She hadn't realized that there was a difference. The second thing she noticed was how rough the walls were. The missing musty smell evidenced there was no water seeping down the walls.

"How did you know about this?" she whispered.

"When I was a young man, about seven years old, I grew bored and started exploring. No one stopped me as long as I got back in time for dinner." He grinned at her. "It was great fun poking around. I explored until I was around ten years old, but by then school was a lot harder and I had to study more, and I grew more interested in what my dad did. I told you about what he does," he said proudly. "He really enjoys being head groom for the horses."

"I'm glad my father didn't know you were down here poking around; he might have thrown you and your parents out of the palace. Now you are the savior in our story."

Willem blushed at her praise.

"Actually, my mother showed all of us the secret passageway from our rooms, but I had never tried to use one of them before. It was dark and scary. I didn't want to go into it. I'm a little surprised that my brothers hadn't either." That thought made her very sad. "If they had more warning, things could have been different."

"Let's just wait until we get you into a less dangerous place. I promise I'll look for your brothers." He led the way until he came to another iron-bound door. He signaled she should be silent. He eased the door open, looking all around. It opened into a tunnel under the stables. He listened at the trapdoor in the ceiling above them.

Princess Leni loved horses and had a special affinity with them. Willem opened the trapdoor and helped her up into the stables. The horses startled at the sudden appearance of someone in their home. She went to calm them and keep them quiet. Willem handed her some treats that were kept by the first stall door. He then moved to the stable doors and listened. Nodding to himself, he opened the door, and they moved out into the courtyard. Two horses whinnied after them, wanting them to come back and visit. The princess looked back before continuing out the door. Keeping in the shadows, they moved along the wall until they got to the postern gate. It was a small gate covered with heavy vines. Willem had always kept it well-oiled when he was young, so it wouldn't squeak. It opened with barely a sound, and they were outside the palace walls and in a dark and damp alley.

"Remind me to oil the hinges for the next trip," he told her, as they looked back at the gate.

The princess looked around with quiet curiosity. She had never been in an alley, and the smell of trash and debris all around surprised her. She wrinkled her nose in distaste and looked down at her shoes. She looked at the pile of manure, used straw, and wet puddles she was walking through. Willem grinned at her, knowing what she was feeling.

"This way," he whispered, as he pointed the way to the end of the alley. There, he flattened himself against the wall of the palace as he peered into the street. It was so late in the day, there were few people around. He didn't see any patrols. He looked back at the girl. She appeared very young, with dirt on her face and clothes. She had on a hooded sweater he pulled up over her face.

"Scared people look down when they are out to do errands. Bow your head and let me do the talking."

She nodded in agreement. They set off, keeping to the shadowy side of the street. Willem walked with the gate of a soldier doing an errand he had to get done. The princess kept her head down like a young person who was being taken somewhere she didn't want to go. They had nearly reached the senator's house before they ran into trouble.

They heard the dreaded words, "Halt, soldier, report." Willem stopped and snapped to attention. A man, also in uniform with a different insignia, came into view. Leni kept her head down, and Willem held his salute.

"You better have a good excuse for being out late, soldier," the officer said.

"Sir, I'm taking a servant girl to the Morje residence, as per orders." He kept his eyes staring straight ahead.

The soldier looked Willem over and walked around Leni. He came to a stop in front of Willem. He took his time looking at them. Finally, he snapped out, "Carry on."

Willem held his position until the officer walked away. He wanted to melt in relief but knew he didn't dare. He said, in a firm voice, as if the stop was the girl's fault, "Come on then. Move quickly." He led the approach to the senator's home. He moved to the side gate and knocked. The gate opened, and they moved through into the garden. He found himself with an armful of woman, Anya. He sighed in relief. "Sorry for snapping at you, Princess. Please hurry. It's almost time for me to report. Oh, sorry. Princess Leni, this is Anya, Senator Aeneas' daughter."

"I know Anya. Thank you for your help," she said. "How is your father?"

"Scared but determined to do what he can. Let's get out of the garden. We don't know who might be watching. Your Highness, we need to take you somewhere secret."

They all moved into the house, where the senator waited.

"My dear, welcome to our home. I'm sorry it is under such dire circumstances," he told her, bowing.

She was a well-trained princess, so she answered, "Thank you, Senator. I hope I don't cause any harm to come to you or yours. Please, call me Leni."

"You honor me and mine."

"Sir, time to report in," Willem interjected softly.

"Leni, could you please stand over behind this door so the scan won't see you? Willem must report soon while he is guarding us and keeping us in the house. General Tariq said nothing about Willem staying in the house. Sloppy of him really." He grinned at her. "Oh, Willem, Anya and I searched the house for surveillance. The only thing we found is the radio that you have to use to report."

Willem nodded in response.

She moved to where he indicated, and the rest took their positions. Willem dialed the scan to the right wavelength and spoke into the monitor, "Report." A face appeared on the screen and said, "Ready."

"Ensign Young reporting in from Senator Aeneas Chin's house, sir. All is well. The senator and his offspring are present for scan."

The soldier touched a button in front of him, and a slight hum sounded. "Report accepted. Report in again in four hours. Out."

The monitor went dark, but everyone stayed where they were. Leni wasn't sure why they didn't move, but she stayed where she was, too, just in case. The monitor gave a brief burp and flickered. Only then did anyone move.

Willem finally signaled that they could move into the other room. They moved into an elegant parlor and collapsed into the chairs and sofas. Leni looked at all of them and noticed how tired they all were.

"They make you report every four hours, day and night, right? How dare they treat you like that? They don't even let you get a decent night's sleep?"

"I'm afraid that is my fault. I forced them into this situation because I didn't want to take the chance the general would assign someone else here," Willem told her in a tired voice.

"What? What right do you have to force them into anything?" the princess demanded.

Anya walked over to Willem and took his hand in hers. Facing the princess, she said, "Your Highness, he didn't have to force us to do anything."

Leni drew in her breath as she stared at them, then slowly nodded in understanding. That explained a lot.

The senator took charge. "Willem, were you able to get in touch with Intergalactic Police?"

"Yes, sir. They said that they would look into it."

"It probably was the best we could hope for, considering we didn't know a specific person to speak to about this. I hope they took your call seriously. Don't worry, son, you did your best, and that's all I could ask. Now, let's talk to our guest. Your Highness, can you tell us what you saw and heard, anything about what has happened to your family?"

Princess Leni suddenly didn't look poised, but more like a young, lost girl. Her eyes filled up with tears and her hands shook. The senator opened his arms to her, and she fled into them. He held her close while she cried.

"I've been so scared. They came in the dark of the night when we were sleeping. Marron and Vrai were in their rooms, and suddenly I heard all kinds of crashing and screaming. I peeked around the door into the hall and saw them being dragged from their rooms. They were bleeding and still trying to fight back. I heard a soldier say they needed to go get the girl, so I ran to the secret dresser, went into the passageway, and closed the door. I listened for a long time and heard them searching, but they didn't know the secret of the passage. Later, I started climbing down the stairs. I went down about three levels and then just sat and cried. That's where Willem found me."

The senator patted her shoulder and looked her in the eye. "You did a very brave thing. When the soldiers searched your room, did you hear them say anything about your father or mother?"

Willem gave a startled gasp that caused everyone to look at him. "I just thought of something, sorry to interrupt."

"No," she continued, "they just kept grumbling that they had to round up the brats. I guess they meant us." Her eyes filled again, and the senator tried to comfort her.

The senator turned back to Leni. "You are doing a great job, and we now know that they took your brothers from their rooms. Anya, why don't you take the princess and get her some supper? Willem and I will be there in a minute."

After they left the room, the senator turned to Willem.

"The queen is still in her hidden location but needs medical help. She had water and food, and I did a field dressing on her, but she will need more soon. I hoped I could look in on her but ran out of time. I will need to return as swiftly as I can, but I don't know where I can move her. She can't come here. She would never survive the trip. That, on top of all the patrols looking for the royal family members, would put her at too much risk, or anyone caught trying to help," Willem told the senator. "I just couldn't think of anything you or Anya could do."

The senator paced as he thought about what Willem had revealed. He didn't like it, but Willem was right. There was nothing he could do at this time to help the queen. At least Willem had done as much as he could to keep her concealed. "Okay, we hope the queen is okay and the three boys are alive, or at least were alive in the recent past. I can't see them dragging the two brothers from their rooms, only to kill them elsewhere. But then, nothing is certain. I'm sure it is Jon that I'm supposed to betray. Tariq wants all the royal family under his control. Maybe he wants something from them. Once he has that, he won't need them anymore, and he will eliminate them. And I think that once I betray Jon, he'll eliminate us as well. We still don't know if the king is alive or dead."

"I agree, sir. We need to help the princess disappear. I'll find a way. I worry about my parents, too, sir. If I disappear, General Tariq might do something to them."

"Okay, this is what we'll do. Contact your parents and have them leave the palace. Do they have a place other than their home where they can go? Explain only enough to get them to cooperate. Do they know the princess?"

"Yes, sir, they are very loyal. They don't have any other place to go. They don't know the princess personally, I don't think, but they love her. I think that when I can go back to the palace to talk with my parents, I can also scout down in the dungeons. Maybe I can find out where the boys are being held."

"That's a great idea, but you need to be very careful. I think I need to take one of my household servants into our confidence and see if he or she can help us. We need someone to take your parents and the princess to seclusion. Unfortunately, Anya and I must stay here for a while longer—not only for the four-hour check-ins, but also in case Jon shows up. The longer we can give everyone to get to safety, the better."

"I understand, sir. I'll contact my parents right away." It disappointed Willem because he had hoped that he, Anya, and the senator could also leave, but what the senator said made sense. Too many disappearances would be suspicious and might jeopardize everyone.

"First, get some sleep. You won't be any good to us when you are exhausted. I'll wake you in time for the next check-in, and then you can go to the palace to talk to your parents. Don't trust the link. I'm sure the general has it monitored somehow."

"Yes, sir."

The senator moved off to talk with the princess and his daughter. Willem gratefully lay down and fell into a deep sleep before the senator was even out of the room. The senator looked back and thought it was a wonder anyone could go to sleep that fast. Shaking his head, he wished he still had that ability, and moved on down the hall.

After the simple meal, he told them about the plan he and Willem had thought up. "Do you mind leaving the city with Willem's parents?" he asked the princess. "We want to get you and them to sanctuary as soon as achievable."

"No, I don't mind except I would like to be here if or when Jon arrives. But I see the need to get Willem's parents to asylum. Willem was very brave, sneaking into the palace." The princess touched Anya's hand and smiled. Anya smiled back.

"Let me make Willem his meal. He should get up soon." Anya set about keeping busy and trying not to think about all the dangers Willem was in every day and night. She felt torn in different directions with wishing she could go with Willem to the palace and help search for the missing royal family members, and knowing she had to stay with her father and Leni to do her part. Sighing in resignation, she started on Willem's meal.

Some minutes later, before she woke him, she just stood and watched him breathe in and out so peacefully. She couldn't resist pushing his hair off his forehead. The slight touch woke him up. He blinked and focused on Anya, and the sight made him smile. His hand lifted to touch her cheek.

"How did I get so lucky to fall in love with you?" he asked. The comment made her blush, and she leaned forward to brush a kiss across his mouth.

"I don't know. How did you get so lucky?"

"I kissed you and nothing was the same. I just knew," he said, looking puzzled. "I didn't know love could happen so fast."

She smiled and gave him another kiss. "Time to get up, and you need to check in, sleepyhead."

"Now you sound like my mother," he complained. She laughed at him and moved so he could get off the sofa.

CHAPTER 22

General Tariq paced in front of the most important machine on the planet. It didn't seem that important to look at it, but this one machine could channel the world's core energy. It was large and ugly looking, made of a mysterious black metal, and it stood out against the gleaming silver of the rest of the room. The table in front of the machine was large enough to hold a grown man but had a strange shape to it, as if they had made it to hold creatures shaped differently than humans. It had a humanoid shape, but the head section had holes to place horns—horns that the king had on his head. Tariq wondered whether Jon had them now. His hand moved to his own head, with its full head of hair. He wondered what he would look like without hair.

The table appeared very alien to his eyes, and he placed his fingers on the surface. Startled, he withdrew it as he felt the surface try to mold to his hand. He knew his planet's history, but it still made him shiver to think of lying on that table. If he wanted that future, he would need to do just that.

"Do you know what this machine is, my dear Prefect?" He didn't wait for an answer. "It is my future and my destiny."

"I have never been in this room before. What does the machine do?"

"How does the world work, do you know, Prefect? Do you remember your lessons from when you were young? Do you remember being told that the king brought forth the physical benefits from the world?"

"Yes, but I didn't understand. I thought it meant that the king distributed the resources."

"That's right, but it is a little more complicated than that. Do you have the disc that I gave you to hold?"

"Right here." The prefect held up the one-inch-wide round disc.

"Put it on the platform."

The prefect, holding the small disc, hastened forward and placed the small chip on the table of the machine. He hurried back to stand at the general's side and, at the irritated look from the general, moved away to the back of the area with the other soldiers. He watched every move the general made. Sensing the power in this room, he dreamed of taking the general's place and taking that power for himself. He doubted he would have the courage or opportunity.

General Tariq impatiently jabbed at the keyboard. A voice rang out loudly in the room. "Please enter the correct code." He waited, and five seconds later, the disc disappeared.

He cursed under his breath. He had expected this but had still hoped. "I need that code," he whispered. "This results from your failure, Prefect. I still need Prince Jon, but I have forgiven you for your failure, and now you will see how I will succeed where you failed."

He turned to the man who still held the second disc. "I will take that for now. All of you go back to the transport chamber and wait for me."

The men hurried to obey, transporting out as promptly as they could. The prefect hesitated and then hastened to follow. He needed better information before he could take on Tariq. For now, he would get his adjutant to gather more information. He dreamed of being King of Tyrea. Yes, he would need better information before he could act.

A KING ASCENDS

Tariq continued to stare at the machine. He now definitely knew he needed a code; he had his verification.

He knew part of the history of how the Tor family got accepted by the machine by picking one member of the family to serve its needs. Connected to the machine, a person could direct the power of the core wherever he or she wanted. He wanted riches, gold, and dominion over everyone. HE WANTED THAT POWER, and he would have it if he had to bleed every person on the planet with even one cell of royal blood.

He turned back to the transporter and started planning his campaign to hunt for more discs. *I'll start with the two brats in the dungeons. Yes, I need those two discs now.*

CHAPTER 23

Willem traveled back into the palace through the same tunnel he had used with the princess, but now he needed to head down the stairs to the bottom where the dungeons were located. He was back to find the two princes. *Let them be alive,* he prayed.

He ghosted down the corridor to the worst cells in the palace. He had learned when he was in school that the palace was a replica of a palace on Earth. It contained all the same features, including an ancient dungeon. Dry and clean, and used for storage, but they were still dungeons, with chains and machines of torture. Determined, Willem vowed to search each one of the many rooms.

Two soldiers moved purposefully through the hallways, so he followed them in the hope that they would lead him to any important prisoners. He looked in all the cells as he followed the soldiers. They passed side passageways with more cells. Willem wondered whether he would have time to check them soon, but right now he was in danger of losing his guides, so he continued to follow the two men. He would have to backtrack if they didn't lead him to the boys. Some cells had grown men in them, and Willem wondered whether they were some of the missing senators. Unfortunately, he couldn't take the time to verify his suspicions.

The guards did not travel quietly but made a fair amount of noise. They laughed at the fun they'd had at the inmates' expense. Willem could smell the alcohol they had been drinking as they moved through the corridors. Willem kept back and hugged the wall so they wouldn't see him as they continued to drink and brag about what they wanted to do to the prisoners. He was getting a bad feeling about all this—the soldiers were drunk, and they didn't seem to need to be quiet or consider what they said. They felt they had permission to do whatever they wanted.

The soldiers stopped in front of a cell, and Willem could hear movement from inside as the men looked in and laughed.

"Hi, little boys. We told you we would be back," the guard said, as he took a drink and passed the bottle to the second guard, who took a drink and looked in the grate at the prisoners.

"Hey, you remember me, don't you little one. Git yourself ready. I'm comin'." He grinned a toothy grin that showed his rotten teeth. "Hurry and git it open. I want to have some fun."

"Okay, okay, I'm git'in it." The first guard stood fumbling with the key to the cell. The sobs and sounds of movement increased in the cell.

Willem wasn't sure what to do. He needed to find the princes, and there was no guarantee that the occupants of the cell were them, but he couldn't leave whoever was in the cell to face the two drunken soldiers.

He moved closer and drew his knife. The guards were so intent on their mission that they paid no attention to anything else. Willem crept cautiously closer.

The first guard finally got the cell door open, and he laughed as he held it open for the second soldier.

"Didn't tink I git it, did ya?" And he made a grand gesture of waving the second guard into the cell. They both fell into the cell. Willem could hear that they were trying to grab the prisoners.

"Got ya, you little bugger," one soldier yelled. A short scream followed by sounds of beating had Willem hurrying forward.

He reached the cell as one soldier fell out of the door. Willem struck him on the head with the blunt end of his knife. *Well, one down, one to go,* he thought. He looked up to see the older boy fighting the other guard. He was giving as well as he was getting, but it was an uneven fight. Even drunk, the soldier outweighed the boy by at least seventy pounds, and the boy was tiring fast. If he didn't get help, it would soon be over, so Willem stepped in to finish it. That chance almost didn't happen. He had forgotten the other boy. He staggered as the smaller boy jumped on his back.

"Whoa, boy, I'm on your side," he yelled, as he continued toward the other guard. With a quick flick of his wrist, he rendered the guard unconscious.

"Can you get off me now?"

The boys gathered to one side of the cell, with the older boy guarding the smaller boy. Willem could hardly believe his eyes or his luck. He saluted, then stepped back and bowed, and the boys stood straighter, but on guard. Willem wondered what the guards had done to the boys during their confinement. He noted the torn clothes and turned to kick the nearest guard in disgust.

"Your highnesses, my name is Willem. Senator Aeneas sent me to find and rescue you. Will you trust me enough to get you to shelter?" He stood and waited for their questions and permission.

"I know you." The oldest boy studied him suspiciously. "You are one of General Tariq's guards."

"Yes, I am, but right now, I'm working for Senator Aeneas and your sister, Princess Leni. We are trying to get you to a hideout. Princess Leni told me to tell you the word, 'lemming.' I don't know the significance of that, but I hope it works."

The two princes stood rigid for a moment and then rushed to him. Their questions poured out, one on top of another.

"Is Leni all right? Where is she? Is she safe?"

Willem held up his hands, and the boys quieted. "She's fine and at the senator's house with him and his daughter. May I ask what does the word 'lemming' mean?" he asked.

"Oh, 'lemming' was the word our parents had in case of trouble. It is lucky Leni gave the word so we would believe you. We have a few hundred questions, sir. If you will answer them, please."

"I will be happy to answer your questions when we are all at the senator's house, but I will give you a quick rundown after we deal with these two." He turned to drag the guards into the cell and find the keys. "Hope they don't get checked on for a nice long time," he said with a grin.

They moved back toward the main passageways, and it surprised Willem how free of guards and people these were. Willem kept looking into each cell as they passed.

"Why are you doing that?"

Willem said gently, "I'm hoping we can find the king. I found the queen and moved her to a fairly camouflaged space, but I will need to get back to her soon. I can't take you to her right now, but I will get her help as rapidly as I can. Do you want to help? Let's all look in these cells and try to find the king."

"We'll help," they said eagerly. With a nod, they also looked in the small windows in the barred doors.

"Where are we going?" Marron asked Willem. He looked into cells as he whispered his question. Vrai also looked at Willem.

"We'll go to Senator Aeneas' house. Do you know him?"

Marron nodded. "Our parents consider him a close friend." At the mention of his parents, his facade cracked a little, and Willem could see tears in his eyes. "He'll know what to do," Marron added, as he shook his head. He raised his chin, eyes glowing with determination. Vrai stepped up next to him, his eyes also showing his determination. Willem marveled at their bravery, and he again bowed to them.

"Well, we better go," Marron said with a small smile.

Willem wanted to check the next level of cells, but he thought the boys could use a little rest, so he started looking for a room where he could hide them and they could lie down for a moment. About ten minutes later, he found what he was looking for in a large supply closet. Cluttered, it attested that few used it, and it was deep enough that the boys could hide under the tarps.

"Here, this will do," and he pulled them into the room. "You can rest under the tarps. Just lie still under these in case anyone comes in." He cautioned them to be quiet. "I have to check the next level of cells, and you need to rest. I'll come back soon." He double-checked that they were settled under the tarps and checked so no one would see them. "I'll be back. Remember, stay silent."

Willem hurried down the hall and up a level to the next set of cells. He checked each cell carefully but didn't see anyone that could be the king, and he didn't see any women at all. He wondered who were all these people that he was seeing. Neither the king nor queen had put this many people in cells. More likely, the general had put them there. He paused as he heard a voice. Moving carefully down the hall, he approached the cell. He saw a man grumbling over and over about the unfairness of it all. Willem listened, hoping he might learn something, but the man just kept saying it wasn't his fault. The world hated him; he was just doing his duty. After five minutes of complaints, Willem was ready to move on, but then the man cried out.

"Damn your eyes, General Tariq!" Then seeming to realize that if anyone heard him, he could get in even worse trouble, the man huddled into himself and sat in the cell's corner. "I didn't let her get away. She just disappeared. She's a witch. She disappeared, I tell you."

Willem wondered who "she" was, but he needed to get back to the boys.

Willem was hesitant to reveal himself to this man because he seemed the type who would use that knowledge to bargain for his freedom. Willem kept checking the cells and thinking about what he had heard. Finding discarded clothes, probably from other prisoners, and a working refrigerator with packed lunches, he grabbed two and bundled some clothing together into a duffel bag he found. He looked like a fresh recruit just reporting for duty. He had to get back to the princes and visit his parents before they could leave the palace. Time was racing away, and there wasn't much of it left with a lot remaining to do.

He hastened down the halls of the dungeon, trying not to draw attention to himself. He was almost to the room when he saw more guards approaching. They were of a higher rank than him, so he saluted till they had passed. They continued on their way with a brief nod. Willem waited until they were out of sight before continuing to the room. Cautiously, he opened the door. Only then did he call out to the young boys.

"Are you here? It's Willem."

They came rushing out of the gloom. "Oh, I'm so glad you're here. We were afraid you wouldn't come back," Vrai gushed in relief.

"Are you okay? Did anyone come in?"

"Yes, we're fine, and one person came in but got what he wanted and left. Did you find any food?" Marron asked hopefully.

"I found a little food and some clothes. I'm not sure how well they will fit, but at least they're clean." He watched as they tore into the food. He wondered when they had last eaten. After all, Tariq hadn't planned to keep them alive.

"Hurry, before someone else comes. Conceal your old clothes back where you had been hiding. We have one more stop to make."

The boys hurried to do as Willem asked and soon were ready to go. They were on the lower level, so Willem led them up several levels and then down the corridor to a small hallway that branched off. This they followed until it dead ended. There were two doors facing each other across the hall. Willem knocked on the one to the left. It opened almost immediately. Willem stood facing his father, who grabbed and hugged Willem before he said a word. Surprised, he returned the hug tightly. Soft giggles came from behind him, and he blushed a bright red.

Stepping back from his father, Willem turned to beckon to the boys. "Sirs, this is my father, Gregory Young, Head Groom of your stables. Father, this is Prince Marron and Prince Vrai. We are in desperate need."

Surprised, Gregory bowed and welcomed them into his home. As they all stepped into the suite of rooms, he gave his son a look that said, "What's going on?"

"Is Mother home?"

"Of course, let me get her." Gregory hurried out and rapidly returned with his wife. "Why are you and the princes here, Willem? What's going on? We hear rumors and don't know what to believe."

Willem could tell that his mother wanted to fuss over the young men, so he asked, "Mom, could you get something to drink for the princes?" When his mom returned with glasses of ice drinks and tea cakes for them, he got down to business while they ate.

"Let's sit down so I can explain. First, we believe General Tariq is making a power grab and has imprisoned or killed the king. The injured queen is concealed for the moment. He imprisoned the princes, and he also tried to grab Princess Leni. I found the princess in the secret passageway from the royal apartments. She had seen the guards grab the princes and ran and hid." Both princes sighed in relief. "She told us about the princes. I found them just a little while ago in the lowest cell in the dungeon. We searched for the king but didn't find him. Please listen to me. It is important that you pack what you can, but take only enough that you can hide it easily. I need you to walk out of the palace like you are going shopping. Instead, I need you to go to the North Market. I'll meet you there. The children and you need to leave the city."

"But…why?"

"They have assigned me to guard the senator. General Tariq is holding them hostage in order to grab Prince Jon when he returns. I have little time left before I have to return to the senator's house. Every four hours I have to report in, and they have to be present. The senator has a plan to get you, the princes, and the princess out of the city. So, please do as I ask."

"Oh, you must come with us," the boys pleaded with Willem's parents. Marron turned solemn eyes on Willem. "What about Jon? Will he be okay?"

Willem looked into the eyes of both of the princes. "I promise to do all I can to keep him unharmed." They nodded understanding.

"Of course, we'll go at once. I can't believe the rumors are true. What a dreadful time. I knew the general was up to no good. Never did like the looks of that man," his mother muttered, as she hurried out of the room. But she was back with more food. "Eat this up. With us gone, it will just spoil."

The princes fell on the food without further urging, and even Willem ate a full plate.

Gregory leaned forward to whisper to Willem. "When do you need to leave?"

"We need to leave in just a few minutes. Father, I love you and mother very much, and I wanted to tell you once again." He hugged him. "Be very careful. There are extra patrols out. Act natural. I'll meet you at the North Market, by the wall. It should be by the second bell. I hate to rush you, young sirs, but we must hurry. We need to go out the secret passageway, and we still have to negotiate the alleys back to the senator's home."

"We're ready. It was very nice meeting you, and we'll see you soon. Thank you for the food."

Gregory bowed. "Good luck and Godspeed."

CHAPTER 24

"Phew, what's that!" exclaimed Vrai.

The princes, like their sister, didn't like the smell of the alley, but since they had spent time in a smelly cell, it didn't affect them as much. They were more amazed by the passageways and kept saying they wished they could have explored more.

"After these troubles are over, you can explore all you want," Willem told them. Even Vrai grinned at that idea.

It surprised them when they didn't run into anyone on the way back. They saw some patrols, but they were far away and didn't look in their direction. The journey to the house proved to very uneventful because the guards sent to kill the princes had apparently not yet been found.

The streets were quiet, and the princes blended into the crowds. Willem found he was the one who stood out the most with his uniform. People shied away from him. He was thankful that he must have seemed to be escorting the two young men somewhere. Although the two boys received sympathetic glances, he really didn't care, as long as they didn't get stopped by any patrols.

"It's going to be close. When we get there, please be quiet until after I check in with control."

The boys nodded; both having matured a lot in a very short amount of time. They'd had a rough time of it lately as they faced down danger, and it showed in how they carried themselves. Willem let them in the side gate and took them into the house when he saw Anya talking to someone. "I'll get Willem right away. He's just with my father."

"He should have answered the door, not you," a gruff voice responded. Willem recognized the voice as his platoon leader. Willem signaled to the boys to hide in the pantry and to be quiet. Seeing them safe in the room, he hurried down a side hallway to the senator's office. Anya saw him and said, in a carrying voice, "Willem, there is a soldier at the door for you."

Willem hurried to the front door. "I was just going to check in, sir. Is there anything I can do for you?" Willem stood at attention.

Sergeant Harper looked down his nose at Willem, obviously hoping to catch Willem away from his post.

"No, I was in the neighborhood and thought I would check that everything was okay here."

"Yes, sir, they have been very cooperative."

The sergeant sniffed. "No sign of the other royal yet?"

"No, sir, we have seen no one yet. I'll report it as soon as we hear or see anything."

"See that you do. I'll just verify that the senator is here as well." He moved purposely to the senator's office and, without knocking, walked right in. Willem quickly made introductions between the two men. The senator barely acknowledged this intruder to his room, and the sergeant stood with his nose in the air.

"Are you satisfied, sir? We have to check in per protocol in a minute." Willem hoped to get the soldier out of the house before he lost his temper.

"Yes, yes, carry on." He stomped out of the room. No one followed him or offered to open the door. The sergeant fumed at the snub.

"That was too close. I almost hit him," Willem whispered to Anya, as she gave him a small kiss. "Let's get the check-in done."

Everyone ran into position, and Willem reported in. After that was over, everyone moved down the corridor to the kitchen pantry where the boys were waiting. Princess Leni launched herself at her brothers, crying uncontrollably. She had almost walked in while the sergeant was in the house, but hearing a strange voice, had hid at the top of the stairs. She ran down the stairs when he left, only to find her two brothers had arrived.

"I was so scared, I thought I had lost you." She hugged them tight. They also were teary-eyed and hugged her back.

"You are both hurt," Anya declared, when she noticed the blood on their faces. "Come, let me treat your wounds." She ushered them to another small room where she had her medical supplies.

The senator took Willem aside and asked where he had found them. Willem told him about the soldiers who were ready to attack them and worse. He said he thought no alarm had sounded because they had not yet found the soldiers.

"That won't last for very long," he said. "The prefect will want to report them so he can redeem himself with the general. Also, I think something is up with the prefect's men. A couple of them were in places they shouldn't be, so something was going on there. My parents have agreed to meet us at the North Market by the wall. I also have bad news. We looked for the king but couldn't locate him in the dungeons. Some cells might house the missing ministers and families. I overheard one prisoner muttering about a woman, but it was very unclear. Something about her disappearing. It can't be about the queen because I know where she is hiding. The king could be in an apartment on one of the upper floors, but my parents had heard no rumors or gossip other than the king and queen are missing. Wait a minute." He turned to the children. "Do you know of any other secret entrances to the passageways besides the chest you used? If you do, we can check there or somewhere else in the passageways for the king."

All three of the children looked thoughtful. Leni was the first to speak. "There was a fireplace in Father's room that had a false back." Marron was next, getting excited. "Also, there is a 'bolt-hole' in Mother's room." Vrai looked stricken that he couldn't think of one to add.

The senator beamed at them. "That gives us some excellent places to look. Now, stay firm, and we'll get out of this mess just fine."

"Okay, the princes can get a bath and into some clean clothes. We'll need to pack some food and some money for them to take with them." Anya organized her first aid supplies as she cleaned a cut on Vrai's cheek. She also put some supplies aside for the group to take with them, just in case.

After the boys had bathed, Anya finished treating their wounds and Leni was busy gathering food that they could hide in their clothing. Willem ran upstairs to grab clothes for Leni from Anya's room. The senator went to his groom's room in the stables to see whether there was anything in the boys' sizes. He soon returned with an assortment of items for them to try on. They did their best to replace the blood-stained clothing with other items that were a little bigger so they could conceal sandwiches and small packets of things, like pickles and cheeses.

Anya set about helping them continue to hide food. The senator came in with some money for each of the children. They didn't want to accept it, but he insisted.

"You will need some money wherever you go. I want you to reach a small estate I own. I have included a map for you. Also, Willem's parents are going with you. I prefer that you all stay together—not only for your protection, but also for theirs. Tariq will probably send patrols out looking for two children, but maybe not for a family of five."

All the children nodded understanding and agreement. Soon, it was time for all of them to leave. Willem changed out of his uniform and departed out the door after everyone hugged goodbye. They filed out of the house one by one and slipped through the side garden entrance. Willem stopped to give them last-minute instructions.

"Stay very close and keep up. We can't take a chance of getting separated, Your Highnesses." Willem looked at each of them. Marron looked Willem straight in the eye.

"Please don't do that. Just use our names," Marron told him solemnly.

"As you wish, Marron." Willem smiled. He liked these kids more and more.

Willem led them through alleys to avoid any patrols on the major streets. As he peered around corners and marched the children down rubbish-filled back alleys, he wondered what the kids thought about their city now. They were certainly seeing a side of it they had never seen before. He looked back at them and noticed the wide eyes and wild stares at the bad smelling debris. He saw Leni wrinkling her nose at the powerful smell coming from some piles that Willem suspected were more than just trash. The boys barely noticed the smell this time.

He watched not only for patrols but also for servants emptying trash, walking dogs, or working in their gardens. He carefully guided them around houses that showed the potential of a lot of activity in the area, like kids' toys or animal pens.

Soon they were near the North Market. Willem stopped them short of the opening to the market before they could be spotted by people passing by. He tried to find his parents before they stepped out of the protecting alleys. Scanning the crowd, noting any patrols and large groups of people, he finally spied his parents standing near the gate. He pointed them out to the children, who were talking among themselves about what to expect.

"Should we pretend to shop and work our way over to your parents?" the boys wanted to know.

"No, I think one of you boys should walk directly to them. Since you have met them, it will look natural. Maybe you should call them Mom or Dad. The patrols are looking for two boys together. Princess Leni, I think you should shop at one stall, maybe buy something small, act like you don't have enough money, just keep your head down, then move over until you get to your brother. Vrai and I will walk over together. Okay?"

They all nodded, and Marron moved out into the crowd. He moved naturally, skirting small groups, and went directly to Gregory and Suri. Willem's parents looked surprised to see him, but soon recovered. Responding to something Marron said, Gregory smiled and clapped him on the shoulder. Leni moved out into the crowd and moved from stall to stall until she found a stall with beautiful combs. She lingered over them for a while and then moved to another stall selling earrings. There she brought a small pair that matched the blue dress she was wearing. Then she acted like she'd just spied Gregory and Suri and moved over to them. Finally, it was Willem and Vrai's turn, but before they could move out of the alley, Willem saw a new patrol enter the market area. He tensed and watched to see what was going to happen.

"Wait." He threw his arm out to keep Vrai from stepping out into the key area. He watched intently to see where the patrol went. They moved purposefully through the crowd and ignored the merchant stalls. Apparently wanting to keep the arrest low-key, the patrol had not come in an air car. They turned into a local bar and returned in a few minutes with the tavern owner in handcuffs. The tavern owner was moving peacefully until he suddenly struggled and screamed that he was being framed. The ruckus drew the eyes of almost everyone in the area. Willem relaxed a little, but only a little. He didn't move himself and Vrai out into the marketplace because there were now other patrols in the square. Vrai's coat had a hood on it, which Willem had him pull up to cover his face. Again, he would be the soldier delivering a servant to a family.

"Okay, hold your head down," he said, and together they strolled across the open area that the patrol had just left. They stopped at a couple of stalls and talked about directions. Finally, they arrived at his parents.

"First part done," he said to his father with a sigh of relief. After surveying the surrounding crowd, Willem moved them a little closer to the gate. They would have to travel on foot for a little while until they could get the tram. That would take them to the main train station. From there, they could travel west to the senator's estate.

Unfortunately, Willem couldn't go with them. He wished he could see them all to a secure harbor. He bade each of them goodbye and wished them a fast and safe trip. He promised them he would keep everyone out of harm. Then he said goodbye to his parents. Saying goodbye, he wanted to go with them, but he couldn't. He had to trust that they would be safely hidden.

"Keep them by you," he told his father and mother, "and please keep yourselves safe. I love you both." And then he disappeared into the crowd.

Gregory gathered Suri to him and looked at the three children, who were watching them with steady eyes. "Okay, let's go. Stay close."

CHAPTER 25

The worried prefect was in a dangerous mood. He hadn't befriended his troops under him. He ruled by fear. His adjutant would do what he instructed him to do, but the prefect wanted to ensure he wouldn't betray him to the general, if it would benefit him. What he needed was someone he could use as leverage against the general. Well, if he couldn't use his adjutant, then he would find someone he could use. He set to work at his desk.

He swiped his hand across his desk to bring up his holo-computer to study his files on his soldiers. Besides the normal information in a soldier's file, he had little bits of information on their families—any negative intel on their lives that could be used to his benefit. Information, supposedly wiped from their files routinely, was still present in his files. He frowned in disappointment when he couldn't find anything he could use. He was fuming inside.

Nothing, not a single thing. Raging against the lack of information, he stalked down the hall to his private room where he had his "special equipment."

The room reflected no light. It was painted totally black. Shackles dotted the wall and chains hung empty to the floor. In the chamber was a black desk and a black chair. He smiled as he moved into the room as a name came to mind. He prided himself that he never forgot a bad comment against him. A crack by one of his soldiers who said he'd always wanted a bar anyway rather than to serve him was the perfect excuse.

"Send Paulo to my private stateroom now." He told the soldier standing outside in the corridor. The man hurried to do his bidding.

Paulo dropped the box he had just picked up as he froze at the announcement.

"Oh man, what did you do?" asked one of his fellow soldiers.

"Can you make a run for it, like maybe to the Southern Continent?" asked another.

He looked at the others in the room and knew he wouldn't make it that far. The others really didn't care what happened to him and would report him missing and where he was likely running to in his effort to escape.

He quickly thought about his options. The prefect kept detailed records on all his men, showing their home areas, relatives, and preferences. Maybe he could hide in plain sight. He did have a little money saved, so maybe he could travel to the north part of this continent, but his fellow soldiers wouldn't let him get far. So, he turned and grabbed his sword and gun and ran. He didn't think his chances were good, but at least he could take a few to the grave with him.

They caught up to him in the lower quarters. They surrounded him. One stunned him, and the others beat him soundly. They didn't want to kill him; they enjoyed the screams too much. They tied him and marched him to the prefect's office. After delivering him, they took bets on how long he would last. The winner took all at four hours and twenty-three minutes. They congratulated him as his body was removed for setting a new record.

CHAPTER 26

Lu-zan took his time touring the space station. He even visited the Visiondeck, where he could look down on the insignificant planet below. It had three major landmasses, two of which were visible through the clouds. The one on the right was the main one that held the Capital, and the one down to the left was a smaller size but had high mountains and a beautiful system of lakes and streams. The third landmass he couldn't see from their present orbit. The planet was a lovely sight. Its oceans and seas were a beautiful blue-green, and it had many islands. It looked like a miniature Earth. Lu-zan wondered where in all that greenery Jon and Alexis were. The clouds obscured the closest major city, and he couldn't see the spaceport at the Capital. From far above, the Capital itself had a curious structural design. Lu-zan could see swirls and beautiful patterns that started at the tip of the central spiral of the castle and continued down to ring the large, crystalline outcroppings that dotted the entire world's surface.

Matt, who had finally arrived, stared down at the breathtaking structure. "Do you know what those crystalline structures do?" he asked Lu-zan.

"Jon told me once that no one knew if they had a function. They were not covered in the history of humans on the planet and so, as far as Jon knew, no one had ever explored them. They had always just been part of the landscape, like the mountains."

"They are beautiful, and so large we can see them from the station. There are so many of them, seems they should have some purpose," Matt added thoughtfully.

"I agree. Well, shall we go?"

They left the deck and made their way back to their quarters. This trip had been successful. Their excuse of getting locations for training had really paid off. They had signed up five new locations from contacts made just at the space station. Who knew what they would find below on the planet?

"How about we try out some of the entertainment venues available on the station?" Lu-zan wriggled his eyebrows at Matt, who rolled his eyes.

"Okay, let's explore," he said, as they walked to the elevator tube. "What level do you want?"

"Any would do."

Matt stepped through the entrance onto the ledge for the down levitation tube and stepped into space as he grabbed the control handle, Lu-zan following him. Together, they floated down five levels through the tube and twisted the handle for level five. As they stepped through the exit, the strobe lighting struck them, cutting through the dim light of the area and the cacophony pounding out of the nearby bars.

"Well, we'll have a great time here." Matt took off toward the first bar he saw, but Lu-zan followed more slowly, looking all around, seeing a seedy district as any he had ever seen. A moment later, he got his answer: a man attacked Matt from the shadows. Lu-zan executed a perfect flying tackle and had the attackers flat in three seconds before Matt ever knew anything was happening.

"Do you still want to visit this establishment?" Lu-zan asked blandly, but Matt shrugged his indifference. "You choose then."

"This way. I think we should visit this one." He led the way towards a bar that was a little more upbeat. He went into a bar with neon pink lights and white furniture that surrounded a raised bar, which rotated slowly. "I like the looks of this one."

They grabbed a table close to the door and about halfway to the bar. When they sat down, a hologram menu lit up on their tabletop. The menu was eclectic, with offerings of pornographic selections mixed in with a variety of religious ones. There were drinks—from tubermilk and Iburion cowmilk to Orion wine, which was said to be the most potent available. After studying the menu, they tapped in their selections. Seconds later, the middle section of the table irised open and delivered their drinks. It contracted shut and disappeared as soon as they picked up their drinks.

Looking around at the clientele, they studied the floorshow taking place in the center section of the revolving bar. A scantily clad female from a far-off planet in the next system over was dancing. Matt thought she was probably from Atea but was not sure. She had an extra joint in her leg that allowed her to move in a way that most humans could not achieve. Matt thought it was interesting to watch, but also a little disturbing, as her limbs moved in ways that didn't seem possible. They slowly finished their drinks as they admired her artistry but soon decided they'd better move on to the next bar. After having a drink at a second bar, they both moved to another elevator tube and went down to another level.

This level was even more crowded, with beings from all over the universe. Here, they found a series of stores that catered to more exotic tastes. Animated tattoos, unusual ingredients, and dangerous, frightening creatures even the two of them were not familiar with were on display. Two of these species included a dog-like creature that spit acid for defense, and a fish that looked like a pterodactyl but flew under water. After looking at a couple of these stores, they continued their descent.

As they continued to descend the levels, they strolled along, gathering information. They moved slowly but deliberately. One or both of them always checked to determine whether they were being pursued as they got nearer to their true destination. Finally, they came to a central courtyard with plantings of flowers and a fountain. Local news vendors sold their rolled up telepads, which could pick up the planetary and intergalactic news. They each bought one and sat at a small table to read the latest news. There, they drank the excellent coffee being sold nearby and waited.

People moved in and out of the square, but one woman came and sat at the table next to them. She also had a telepad and some of the wonderful coffee. She stayed only a little while and then got up to leave.

"Oh, I'm sorry, excuse me," she said, as she accidentally bumped Lu-zan's chair. He got up, but she insisted. "No, no, please don't get up, I can get by. Thank you."

Lu-zan bowed in his chair.

Matt watched it all happen with a bemused smile on his face until he noticed Lu-zan palming a small plexitext. The pass was quick, and no one else noticed the small sheet. They stayed awhile and casually had another coffee before they moved to return to their rooms. The trip up the elevator tube was uneventful, and they didn't stop until they reached their rooms a few minutes later. Both of them were eager to read the message. They weren't expecting much news from this agent, but they read with great interest.

The plexitext had several points of interest listed. One item struck them as particularly ominous. General Tariq had gotten a couple of his men into positions of importance on the space station. The positions they held would give them access to transports at crucial times. The kidnapping of Jon had apparently been a long-planned event. General Tariq's nefarious resources made him a very dangerous man—not just to this planet but also to the neighboring ones. He could reach out to take over other planets in this system using the resources of Tyrea. He had to be stopped, and Matt hoped that Jon's plan could do the job.

The last part of the message brought a ray of hope. The station manager was aware of the problems on Tyrea and had been watching for a move on the general's part to place people on the station.

The station manager was keeping a tight watch on the agents and would remove them from power if he could. He had placed his own agents with each suspected spy. Both hoped that each of these agents remained undetected. Each agent would continue to monitor the situation and would send for help if necessary. That was all they could do without probable cause for now.

Mission complete, it was time to move to the planet's surface. They packed their bags to prepare for going planet side first thing in the morning. They had a leisurely meal at a nearby restaurant and went back to their rooms for a good night's sleep.

CHAPTER 27

Jon and Alexis, now free to move around, hurried into the surrounding greenery of the forest lands.

"Let's check our disguises," Jon said. He turned to inspect Alexis' disguise. She turned slowly in her hat, which shielded her eyes from the sun. The dress she wore was a little big and helped to hide her slim figure, and the hiking boots were sturdy and didn't look shiny and new.

"Your turn," she told him.

Jon dutifully turned for her inspection. She stepped forward to straighten his wig and tugged a little on his shirt so it hung lopsided. His boots also didn't look new.

"I think we should follow the tree line, in case of any air patrols. Plus, we shouldn't light any fires. We don't want to attract any unwanted attention to ourselves," he said, and Alexis nodded agreement.

The space port was on the southern coast, close to the city of Glenn, the founding city, and they needed to reach the capital, about fifty miles inland. All of them had discussed sending their container to the space port next to the capital but had vetoed that idea because of the danger of recognition by Tariq's stationed agents, who they were sure would be there. Jon also didn't dare try to rent an air car or get train tickets for the same reason, so they planned to travel on foot. Jon figured that if they traveled four miles an hour, it would take them about twelve to fourteen hours to get there. Their goal was two days of travel time.

They made good time for a while, but after a couple of hours, Jon noticed that Alexis was slowing down. They had traveled cross-country, trying to avoid farmhouses and open, inhabited areas. Jon realized, though she didn't complain, she certainly was not used to this test of endurance.

Jon stopped, causing Alexis to go on alert.

"Are you all right?" she asked.

"Just a little tired. I thought maybe we could take a brief break."

"Sounds good to me. I'm not used to this much walking, especially over rough terrain. I'm used to flat hospital corridors."

Jon smiled at her and looked her up and down. "You look like you work out."

"I didn't say I didn't exercise, I said I'm not used to walking in the woods."

Jon put his hands up in mock surrender. "Let's stop here for a few minutes to catch our breath."

Alexis pulled out some of the various food items Lu-zan had packed for them, laughing as she held up the two carefully wrapped packages she had opened. Each contained one dessert that Lu-zan loved so much.

"Wow, I'm surprised he gave up two of those. What else is in there?" Jon asked, as he took one of the opened packages.

"Let's see, there is some meat and some strips of what I think is a vegetable. Want to try it?"

"Sure, I have had worse. Mmm, that's good, try some, I think you'll like it."

"You're right, that is good," she said, as she chewed the vegetable. "I think when we're done, we should ask Phillip's wife for the recipe."

After they finished their small meal, they moved on through the forest. Jon told Alexis about his world as they walked along.

"We are basically an agrarian society. The settlers who crashed on the planet had to deal with survival first. One of the first things they needed to do was plant crops. They had little supplies that survived the crash, but they were fortunate. They salvaged some stored seeds and sedated livestock from the ship. The planet had compatible soil, and the harvest was plentiful that first season. They built well with the stone, and the colony flourished. At first, they could only support themselves, but later, when the population had grown, they diversified into trades. Now we grow enough to support ourselves and still export some valuable crops off planet. There isn't much in seismic activity, and what takes place doesn't happen where people are living. The weather is glorious all over the planet, although we have seasons. We have modest icecaps, but overall, the temperatures stay between 10 to 100 degrees. We are lucky that the view of the planet is in a favorable zone, in terms of distance from the sun, so what more can you ask for?" He stopped. "I feel I have been doing all the talking. I want to learn about you."

"There is so much more I want to learn since we're here. I promise I'll tell you all about me later, okay? What about mining or manufacturing? Will I be able to buy a souvenir of my time on Tyrea?"

"I'm sure we can come up with something for you, and to answer your question, we have little mining. The planet was only settled for a couple of thousand years, and they have found most of the manufacturing resources close to the surface and easily accessed," he commented. "Earth went from basic agrarian to being technically advanced within twelve thousand years. I think we haven't because we already had a lot of technology with us and found we didn't need all of it, but it's still there if we need it."

The first day they made good time, despite the rest breaks, and Jon estimated they were about halfway to the city. Jon kept a close watch for air patrols. At dusk, they stopped for the night. They gathered wood and stones and made camp. Alexis dug out some more of their food and set out the campfire canister that made a small ball, which gave off an adjustable heat and light. They shielded this small light behind some boulders. The food came in small containers that warmed the food automatically when activated. Together, they enjoyed their meal as they each lay on a small blanket they had brought, propped against the rocks, watching the beautiful sunset.

"Tell me some more about your world. It's so beautiful."

"Well, it's small, about two-thirds the size of the prison planet. And we have three major continents, with two polar icecaps, north and south. There were no large predators on the planet when we first came here. The crash was awful and had disabled the ship, but lucky for us, there were seed vaults and animals being held in deep hibernation. They found a few planetary species that were well hidden." Jon smiled in memory. "There is a rabbit-like creature that is so friendly, it can become a nuisance if you let it, and a lovely horse-like creature that is very shy. Both of them are herbivores."

"Tell me about your parents," she asked, watching him. Jon was silent for a long time, and then he spoke.

"My mother would love you. Like you, she can be impulsive." He smiled, kidding her. "She is very strong and funny, and she adores my father." He suddenly stiffened as he thought about what he had just said.

Alexis had never thought of herself like that, and she gathered a little closer to him. "What does a queen do on your planet, especially if the position is honorary, like you said?"

Jon looked away from her, as if he were deciding what to say. Finally, he said, "It is not really honorary. She appears with my dad at functions and when he has to give a yearly report on the status of the planet's energy or visit the representatives from the other continents. He always works for the best interest of the planet and people, and he is the only one with direct access to the planet's energy resources, although no one seems to understand how it works, but they have to do with the physical changes he has undergone—and now I have undergone, too."

Jon fell silent, thinking about those changes and their implications.

He seemed so sad, so she tried to change the subject a little. Even though she had a million questions to ask him, she wanted to keep it light.

"Sounds like a straightforward job to me. Do your parents have time for each other or any hobbies or interests they share?"

"Mom does. She loves to teach, and travels to encourage education for everyone, and you are not getting off that easily. Next time is your turn to tell me about you."

"Where are all the people? I mean, shouldn't there be activity in some of these fields?" she asked.

"It does seem odd, not to see anyone else. If Tariq has patrols flying, maybe the citizens are staying close to home," he murmured. Her question did make him uneasy. He wondered whether the city would be as deserted. That would make getting to the senator's house a lot harder.

They talked easily for a while longer until resting for the night. Jon got two sleeping bags out that instantly expanded into comfortable pads. They settled on them and were soon asleep.

When they set out the next day, Alexis hoped Jon knew where they were going. She wasn't used to hiking, and she worried about Jon's overall condition. Even though he appeared fine, he had gone through such a series of traumatic experiences, there must be some residual damage.

Jon had trouble once when he thought he could take a shortcut and went over a fence, only to face a very territorial and very large bull about halfway across the field. It had huge horns that corkscrewed out on both sides of its head. Alexis, who had just climbed the fence, saw the bull come out of a small treed area behind where Jon was walking.

"Jon," she yelled, as she jumped back off the fence. "Run, run!"

The bull didn't want to share his pasture, especially with another male. Jon barely made it over the fence, and he turned and bowed to the bull, who puffed in disdain and trotted away, causing Jon to hold his sore side and fold in laughter. It took a while for Alexis to run around the fenced area. By the time she got there, she had a few choice words for Jon.

"Are you crazy? You terrified me!" she yelled at him, as she stormed up. Jon panted and laughed, almost choking as he stared at the bull pawing the ground. Alexis insisted they stop for a few minutes so she could inspect his wounds to ensure that they hadn't re-opened. He seemed healed, but she didn't trust something she really didn't understand. She was a doctor, and what had happened to Jon defied her understanding. She was very thorough in her examination, and though the wound proved to be sore to the touch, it had not re-opened.

"Seriously, Jon, I don't understand what that cocoon did to you. Something like that could really help advance medical science immensely. Can you explain it to me further?"

"I wish I could, but it is something normal for my family. Maybe someday I'll understand it more, and I promise I will explain it to you." He worried that if she realized the implications of everything, she would run screaming. He feared that he really cared for her, and he didn't want to scare her away.

They continued to travel with frequent stops. If they saw people working in their fields, they traveled around them. They didn't make fast progress, but they also met no more obstacles in their path.

Alexis took time to ask about the beautiful blossoms that surrounded them. One in particular took her breath away, as they stepped out from under the forest canopy. The tiny open area was covered in purple blooms.

"Oh, Jon, it's so lovely. What are they called?"

"I don't know, but I'll find out the name as soon as I can," he answered.

As they walked through the field, they noticed the wonderful scent that drifted up from their footsteps.

"I wouldn't mind having some perfume made from them," Alexis declared, as she took a deep breath.

Jon smiled at her as they shared this magical moment. It made him happy to give her such a memory.

Finally, they were approaching the edge of the city as dusk settled gently on the landscape. Jon could feel his reluctance growing as the end of the trip came into sight.

"It's a beautiful city, Jon. So big! This is the capital for the entire planet?"

"Yes, it is, but the other continents have capital cities, too. They just don't decide for the entire world. It's a little complicated as a system, but it works. Do you see the palace on the hill?"

"I see it. It's like a fairy castle!"

Alexis saw the many soaring towers and crystalline arcs. The tallest tower had a large, crystal teardrop with a single flag flying. The base of the castle had elevated petal-shaped landing pads with larger matching parking areas spaced beneath. City roads spread out in gentle curves, which completed the illusion of a flower blooming from the top of a small hill.

"Some photographs of fairy castles they saw in an old book of theme parks inspired the original settlers. It is beautiful, but it's hard to update the technology every hundred years. We have tried to keep the original exterior as intact as possible. The planet provided an interior scaffolding with air-travel tubes. These supplied the castle builders with a blueprint for the exterior."

"Let's go. I can't wait to see more. Where is Senator Aeneas' house located?"

"We won't have to go around the palace grounds to get to his home. It's a lot closer than that." Again, Jon felt his reluctance to end the peaceful journey. He knew they needed to get to the senator's house as rapidly as possible, but he dreaded what lie ahead for him. Jon knew this peaceful interlude with Alexis was coming to an end.

Jon led the way through alleys and around houses on the outskirts of the city. After that, they walked through a warehouse area where all the grain storage was held, and the smell and sheen of grain dust filled the air. Large, imposing buildings came into view as they entered the business area. Jon and Alexis skirted these because of the increase in people in the area. Jon was careful to keep his head covered for fear of anyone recognizing the telltale traits of his transformation.

As they got closer to the markets and smaller businesses, they noticed that there were fewer people. One section had Jon redouble his efforts to cover his face and head, but his luck ran out when a passerby recognized him. Jon turned away, but the man calmly put his arm around him and spoke into Jon's ear.

"Jon, it's me, Evin. You need to stay away from the patrols." Evin leaned in so Jon could see his face. Jon relaxed somewhat but remained alert. "Come with me for a minute. You will be protected, I promise you." Jon and Alexis reluctantly followed Evin to a store, just as a patrol swung into the street. Evin led them into the back room and closed the door.

"Patrols have increased recently, and they are stopping all the people on the street. We think they're looking for you. Rumors have circulated that you were returning, and everyone has been on the lookout for you. Jon, you have many friends in the city who want to help. What do you need us to do?"

Jon was feeling overwhelmed by everything that had happened in the last week—from the attack, the careful course they had traveled, and now to this welcome. His head whipped up in disbelief when he heard Alexis say, "We have to get to Senator Aeneas' house. And then we have to go to the palace."

"Alexis!" Jon whispered.

"Well, we do, and if your friend can't help us, then we'd better get going." Alexis looked hopefully at Evin.

Jon also looked at Evin, who grinned and spread his hands. "You've come to the right place. What a lucky break. Stay here."

Jon turned to Alexis. "Why did you tell him that? I was thinking of a perfectly plausible lie. I don't wish to endanger anyone else."

"Well, we are all endangered, Your Highness," Evin said, as he and four others came into the room. "We are all loyal to your family, and we want to help. It has been a long time, and perhaps you are also out of touch, but rumor is your father, mother, sister, and brothers are missing. I know it may be harsh to hear, and I apologize, but you need to know. Let us help you find them and right this wrong."

Jon looked at all of them. He shook his head, then lowered his head covering and wig to reveal his loss of hair, which caused some of them to sharply intake their breath. Jon said softly to them all, "You humble me, friends. I gladly accept your help. We need to go to Senator Aeneas' house. Can you help us without endangering yourselves?"

"Your Highness, we will be very careful, of you, and of ourselves. What was your plan, if we can ask?"

"We were going to travel the alleys to get close to the senator's house and go into the garden from the side gate."

"Your Highness, why do all that when we can deliver a package to the senator of some new kitchenware he had ordered? If he has company, he is simply receiving something he ordered anyway. Would that work?"

Jon smiled. "That would work. Evin, call me Jon, old friend."

Later, Jon and Alexis climbed into a large box marked, "Breakable." Alexis looked at the box and sighed. "You know, this is becoming a habit." The top lowered and secured as they held hands.

The group of men carried the box out to the air car, along with several other deliveries. Evin saw a patrol who were asking everyone they stopped if they had seen any strangers on the street.

Lucky I found Jon and Alexis when I did, Evin thought.

The patrol was not paying any attention to the normal activity of the stores, and deliveries seemed to be made unmolested. Two of the men climbed into the air car with Evin, and they took off to make their routine deliveries. They drove at a leisurely rate and made their regular deliveries at several locations, and he took a little extra time at certain locations to tell them Jon was back. Finally, Evin arrived at the senator's home and went to the back door to make the delivery.

Willem opened the door, and Evin pulled back in dismay. He had not expected a soldier dressed in Tariq's livery to answer the door here. He took a sharp breath and announced that he had a delivery for the senator. Willem told him to stay at the door and went to get the senator. Anya and her father both appeared a few moments later, accompanied by Willem.

"Just delivering your new kitchenware, sire." Evin nodded to both of them.

"I ordered nothing, especially kitchenware. Take it back, I don't need it."

"But sire, you will want this kitchenware. It has come from a very long way. Let me open it so you can see."

"I ordered nothing and none of my staff ordered anything, I tell you."

"Yes, I mean, no, sire. Just look at it. You'll be glad you did."

"Father, let the man show us the wares." Willem and Anya moved to the side to let Evin and his helper carry the box into the kitchen.

"My, that is a big box. How much kitchenware did you buy, Father?"

"I didn't buy any kitchenware," he huffed out in protest. "Are you sure there is no mistake?"

"No, sire, there is no mistake." He began to open the box but stopped and asked whether Willem could help him with something in the air car. Willem agreed, and they went out to the vehicle. Evin gave his helper a significant glance. The helper finished opening the box and told the occupants to hurry. Jon had taken off his disguise and hesitantly stood up. Holding Alexis' hand, they stepped out of the container.

The senator and Anya watched with their mouths open in astonishment as Jon and Alexis stood there, wondering where they could hide. This was not the way they had thought Jon would arrive.

"Jon, is that you? You are the very image of your father!" Then he realized what he had said, abashed. "Oh, Jon, I'm sorry." He rushed to embrace the young man. "We've missed you. Welcome home, Your Highness."

Both he and Anya wondered about the identity of the woman with him, but it had to wait until Jon introduced her. Jon and Alexis moved to hide in another room, with Jon giving the senator a quick squeeze of the arm as he passed him.

"You don't need to worry about this officer, Jon. His name is Willem, and he is on our side. I'll introduce you when he returns with Evin. Wait, please, and we'll have introductions all around."

Jon nodded but said nothing. Instead, he began some stretching exercises to loosen his sore muscles, which were stiff from being in a box again. Alexis followed his example.

Willem and Evin came back inside, and it surprised Willem to see Jon and Alexis in the room. Evin turned and pushed the surprised Willem against the wall, reaching for his gun. Chaos erupted, and everyone started yelling at Evin to stop.

"Evin, stop. Let him go. He is not the enemy." The senator's roar surprised everyone. "Evin, please, let him go, and I'll explain." The senator outlined how Willem had taken steps to help find the royal family and get them to refuge, and how he was playing a dangerous game with Tariq. Finally, he explained that Anya and Willem were in love.

"Father!"

"Well, you are, so why deny it. We don't have time."

Jon laughed and relaxed. He looked at Alexis and at a blushing Anya and Willem.

"May I introduce Dr. Alexis Michaels, who is my doctor and hopefully, my love."

"Jon!"

"Well, you are, and he's right. We don't have time." He turned to the others. "Thank you, Evin." Turning to the man who had helped, he said seriously, "I'm sorry I don't yet know your name, sir, but I promise to remember your help for my entire life, be it long or short. We wouldn't have made it here without you. If everything works out, we will meet again. If not, then thank you with all my heart."

Evin and his friend bowed to Jon, shook hands with everyone, and turned to leave. At the door, he turned back to Jon and said, "His name is Kel. He and I are with you, along with all the people, Prince. May the Creator be with you."

"Thank you, old friend," Jon said to Evin, who grinned.

After they had left, Willem reminded them about their next check-in, and at Jon's quizzical expression, they explained about Tariq's threat. It appalled Jon that he had put his friend in such a dangerous situation because of him. The senator dismissed his concerns.

He told Jon bluntly, "Tariq is insane, and nothing you could have done would have changed things. It's obvious that the planet is calling you. We will talk after the check-in," he said. As everyone moved into position, Jon and Alexis hurried to a hiding place.

Later, Jon told him, "Senator, the changes came on me after the general had me kidnapped as my team was setting up camp. I was injured and being transported back to Tyrea by the prefect, when our ship developed a problem and crashed onto the prison planet called Greenwich. My body responded with protective webs over the worst injuries. The prefect demanded my release for the trip back to Tyrea. Alexis helped me escape, putting herself and her staff in danger. It entailed traveling by river, and the water triggered a protective cocoon made from the same material as the webs. Alexis can tell you about the next part of the journey. When released from the cocoon, the changes had already started. Senator, I know my father is dead. I felt his death, or at least I felt he must be near death.

What else would trigger the changes in me?" Jon spoke in a soft voice.

"Willem helped your mother and is still searching for your father, so there is still hope for him. Willem has already sent your siblings and his own parents to a hideout. Please, try to relax a little, and know we won't stop until we get some answers."

Anya interrupted. "Alexis, are you hungry?"

Alexis' answer was her stomach growling. Everyone laughed companionably.

Anya hurried into the kitchen, but everyone followed her and gathered around the island in the midst of the room. They shared sandwiches made with anything that was in the refrigerator or storage units. Jon rubbed his stomach as he realized he had eaten more just now than he had in the last three days. He looked at the contented look on Alexis' face and knew she felt the same.

The senator shooed them off to bed, since they were dead on their feet. Jon and Alexis both climbed the stairs to two bedrooms. There, they barely got their shoes off before they fell onto the beds. Downstairs, the senator, Anya, and Willem prepared to check in again.

While Jon and Alexis slept upstairs, Willem and Anya cleaned up the kitchen and got the box out of the room and into the storeroom. There was a lot of dropping the box and touching as they picked it up again. Laughter sounded from the kitchen, while in the living room the senator sat alone and worried. He wondered how they would get Jon and Alexis into the palace, and what part Alexis had to play in this game. Worried about whether he would see his friends, the king and queen, or Jon's siblings again, he especially wondered whether they would stop the general.

CHAPTER 28

Gregory and Suri led the way on the long walk to the tram station. Suri used the time to talk with Leni, and they had a great time comparing clothes and jewelry. Gregory marveled at how skillful Suri was at distracting Leni from thinking about all that she was leaving behind. He looked at the boys and realized that his job would be a lot harder. Marron was older and was the most aware of the consequences if caught. Vrai, though, had been in that cell with Marron when Willem found them. He also wouldn't be fast to forgive or forget the terror and battering they had endured from those guards.

"Anyone need a rest?" Gregory asked, after they had walked a little farther and he had spied a handy bench. They had come about two miles according to the map supplied by the senator and had about one more mile to go to the tram station. Suri and the children settled on the bench, so Gregory took the time to consult the map.

"Is that the map the senator was talking about, sir?"

"Yes, indeed. Would you like to look at it? As you can see, we have about a mile to walk to the tram station, and then we take the tram to the train station, and then on to the estate." He handed the map to Marron, who studied it intently. Gregory liked this young man, and he could tell that Willem liked him, too.

"I used to love to study the old maps in the library. Father said I showed promise as a cartographer." He handed the map back sadly. "I miss him so much."

Gregory remembered when his father had died, how lost he had felt. "We know nothing for sure, so keep remembering him and your memories in here." He tapped the young man's heart as he continued to speak. "He'll know it, if he is alive or dead. No matter what, hold him close."

Marron thought about that for a moment and smiled shyly at Gregory. "Thank you, sir. That helps."

Soon, they set out again and covered the remaining mile. They were on time for the tram and boarded immediately. It was a quick trip to the larger train station, where they disembarked. The train was leaving in a few minutes, and they hurried to get their tickets and get onboard.

During the trip, they took advantage of a few minutes to eat and drink something. The train was one of the newest designs that never touched the rails; it rode above them, so it was very smooth. It was called an air-rail. The group sat reading all the literature that was in the pocket in front of their seats. Gregory talked with them about the physics involved in the train's construction. Worn out, Suri and Leni soon were dozing in their seats. A few minutes later, Marron and Vrai joined them in sleep. Gregory sat in his seat and thought about fathers and sons. He hoped he would see his son again. Looking at each of the sleeping children, he prayed they would see their parents again, too.

The senator's estate was several miles from the train station in the small village of Sexton-on Avon, named for a small village in England on Earth. It had the same quaint look that the history books showed the original to have had. Gregory rented an air car to fly there, and all admired how beautiful the little cottage was in the small clearing where it nestled. Nestled was the only word for it. Flowers surrounded the house. Everywhere they looked were blooms of roses, daisies, and other plants not from Earth. Suri only knew a few of the names, but Leni could name almost all of them.

They parked the air car and walked up the flower-lined sidewalk to the front door. Gregory tapped in the code that Senator Aeneas had given him, and the door opened. Relief swamped the group. They had made it, but not wanting to assume that they were out of danger yet, they crept into the home. Gregory and Suri moved farther into the house to see what was there. Gregory moved up the stairs to count bedrooms, and Suri moved to the kitchen and dining room. Both returned to the main room and sat down on the well-used, cushy furniture and smiled.

"Well, we should be comfortable. There are five bedrooms and three baths upstairs."

"And we'll eat well. There is a deep freeze the size of a small city in the kitchen and a pantry with every kind of flour, salt, and sugar I can think of," Suri added to Gregory's summary. "The refrigerator is full of food. The senator must have sent workers to stock up ahead of time. Bless the man."

Gregory and Suri gathered the children together and got them upstairs and sorted into the bedrooms. Each had a choice of one of their own, but Marron and Vrai stayed together. They were asleep before the grown-ups were out of the rooms. Gregory and Suri then took themselves off to the bedroom they were going to use for their own. They barely got the words, "Good night," out before they, too, were fast asleep.

CHAPTER 29

Evin and Kel arrived back at his shop only to find it full of friends and neighbors. Surprised, Evin soon learned that all his friends knew he had taken the prince to the senator.

"Hetti, that was supposed to be kept quiet. We don't want to put the prince's life or anyone else with him in more danger."

"Nonsense. Everyone here is loyal to him and his family. That's why we are here. We want to help."

"Hetti's right, we want to help," Sam, the pharmacist from next door, said in defense of his neighbor.

"What do you think you can do? The prince is going to the palace, and he has a plan. That's all I know," said Evin, as he looked at everyone there. "We don't want the plan ruined because we did the wrong thing. I know all of you support our king and queen, but I can tell you that Jon has gone through the change. You know what that means. Our king is dead…long live the new King Jon."

"The king is dead?" someone shouted.

"Please, people, quiet. We don't want to alert the patrol. We could organize, so if or when they need us to do something, we'll be ready."

"How can we do that?" Torren asked. He was the owner of the grocery store next to Evin's shop.

"Well, how about some way to contact one another for starters, like those wrist communicators you have in your store, Blake?"

"I don't have enough of them for everyone, but if we formed groups, I could supply one per group. Also, I think one should go to the prince, err I mean, the king's party so they can communicate with us."

"That's excellent. Let's form up into groups. I suggest that neighbors group together, that way news will travel faster. Blake, can you go get those communicators now so we can distribute them right away?" Evin turned to talk to Kel when he spied out of the window a patrol just coming down the street.

"Patrol heading this way. Everyone look busy. Look at the stock or something, act as natural as you can." He picked up a fry pan and said, just as the patrol walked into the store, "Let me wrap this up for you. Only take a minute." Evin turned to move back to the counter, only to find a patrolman standing in his way.

"Why are so many people here?" a soldier demanded.

"Good day to you, sir. I'm surprised also. I had just received a new shipment of a new style of fry pans. Word must have leaked. Why, I didn't even have time to make fresh signs for the windows and displays. Would you like to see them?"

"No, I don't need a fry pan. This crowd should disperse. The general doesn't like too many people congregating together."

"But I'm an honest business owner, and these are my customers! How can I control how many can be in a store at one time?"

"You better manage it, I'm warning you."

"Well, thank you for the warning, sir. Will you excuse me while I wait on this customer?"

The young soldier stared hard at Evin, not wanting to show his lack of leadership as the new squad leader. He shook his head and signaled to the patrol to move out. A sigh of relief sounded as the patrolmen reluctantly left the store.

Evin wrapped the fry pan up and gave it to Blake. "Go get the communicators and come through the back way so they don't see you. We won't have much time, considering the general is dictating how many people can get together. Soon, we will have a full-blown dictator on our hands."

Blake nodded sagely and left. Everyone else grabbed minor items to purchase, and Evin wrapped them. Some even purchased fry pans. Evin said nothing. He just wrapped the items up as they all stalled for time. Blake returned through the back door with the communicators, and they made quick work of disbursing them to the smaller groups. Evin took two—one for him and one to get to Jon.

"Blake, let me know how many of these you gave us and how much they cost. I'll cover your expenses," Evin whispered to his friend.

Blake looked surprised at the offer and declined. "We are all in this together. No need to cover my expenses, my friend. I do this for my world."

"Okay, everyone, as soon as I hear any news, I'll communicate it to you through this. I'll use channel three. Other groups can use the other channels. Good luck, everyone and be careful." His friends left the store in groups of two or three at a time. In a few minutes, there was only Hetti and him remaining. She gave him a brief pat on the cheek and went into the back room where the entrance to her apartment upstairs was located.

Evin wrapped one more pan and locked his store. He took the alleys in order to move more quickly, and he wanted to avoid any patrols that were out. He had a feeling that events were going to happen soon, and he wanted to be ready to help if Jon needed him.

Evin remembered the first occasion he had met the prince. He was eight years old and always getting into trouble. One day he was running in the alleys and looking into the trash cans because people threw out the most interesting things. He heard a noise and went still. After all, it could be a rat or the owner of the rubbish can. He heard it again. No, couldn't be the owner of the rubbish can because they would have already grabbed his belt and pulled him from off the rubbish. Must be a rat, but he couldn't see it. He backed out of the can. When he stood up, he caught a brief flash of something running past him. He twirled around and saw a small figure dash behind a large crate. He walked over and peered around the crate. There was a small boy, younger than him by a couple of cycles.

"Hi," Evin said to the small boy.

"Hi," answered the boy.

"What are you doing here?"

"I'm lost," the young boy answered truthfully.

"Where do you live?"

"In the palace, and my mother is going to kill me."

Evin could see the boy was close to tears. "Nah, mothers don't do that, but we'd better get you back. What's your mother do at the palace?" Evin expected to hear she was an upstairs maid or something like that.

"She's the queen."

"Ha-ha, no what does she do?"

"I told you, I don't lie. I'm a prince, so she's the queen."

"Okay, if she's the queen, what's her name?"

"Mother, of course."

"No, I mean, like her name. Mine's Evin, and your name is…?"

"Oh, my name is Jon. My mother's name is Queen Lenore."

Okay, thought Evin. He knew the Queen's name was Lenore. He wondered, *What if this is Prince Jon?* As they moved though the alleys, he asked, "How did you get out of the palace?"

"Oh, Mother told me about a secret passageway to use in case of trouble in the palace, and I was curious. I walked and walked and then I couldn't find my way back. I opened a door and was outside. So, I walked around looking for the front, but didn't find it. Now, I don't know how to get back. Can you help me?"

"Sure," he answered, even as he thought about what he could do. He could let his parents handle it, but that would lead to how he'd met Jon in the first place, and he would get in trouble for getting into trash cans. Or he could try to take the prince home himself. He decided he would take the prince home so neither of them would get into trouble.

Now, Evin knew the general direction of the front of the palace. After all, it was that huge crystal and stone building. How hard could it be to find the entrance, right? So, he took the prince's hand, and they set off. Evin reasoned that since he had been in an alley, the front should be in the opposite direction, toward the major streets. So, they walked and walked. Evin was hesitant to ask the people they saw on the street because he didn't smell very good after being in the trash. He saw soldiers marching, so he pulled Jon that way. The soldiers marched into a wide palace gate to the north, so he pulled Jon after him as he peered inside the gate. They could see lots of soldiers and people milling around a large door. They all seemed to be in a great hurry and very agitated. Jon watched all the activity with very wide eyes. Then they widened even more with relief, and he cried out.

"Mother!" Jon tore his hand out from Evin's and started running across the courtyard. Everyone stopped and turned to see Evin standing there with his mouth hanging open and Jon running toward a tall woman who had been crying. Evin turned to go, but a big hand descended onto his shoulder, pinning him in place. Now petrified, he was thinking he was REALLY going to be punished. Re-united, mother and son had a tearful hug, and the hand marched Evin across the courtyard toward them.

"Mother, meet my new friend, Evin. He helped me come home."

Queen Lenore turned to Evin and gave him an enormous smile. "Thank you, young sir, for bringing my son back to me. Let me repay you for your kindness. Is there anything special you would like that I can get for you?"

Evin bowed or tried to, but with the man's hand still on his shoulder, he couldn't quite move properly. The queen smiled at the man holding him. "I think you can let go now, dear." The hand withdrew, but then the words penetrated Evin's brain, and he twirled around to stare up into the eyes of the king. Jon smiled up at his father.

Evin stammered, "Your Highnesses." He bowed as carefully as an eight-year-old boy could. "I don't need a reward. I was just bringing him home like he asked me to."

The king, smiling down at them, said, "Home from the alleys, I take it from the smell."

Evin blushed and backed away. "Sorry."

"No, no need to be sorry, son. I played there also as a child. Let's go in and get you cleaned up."

Evin found himself marched into the palace. Soon, the king and queen had invited his parents to come to the palace. While they waited for them to arrive, they sent for clothing for both children. They also had the boys take baths and get cleaned up. Evin tried to look at everything so he could describe it later to his friends and parents. When his parents arrived, looking like they wanted to melt into the floor, they all sat down for a private dinner. Jon's parents charmed Evin's, and soon they were all laughing and having a good time, relaxed around a sumptuous dessert.

"Evin has proved to be a wonderful companion for Jon," the queen told his parents, "and we hope he can come and join us again in the future."

Thrilled, Jon laughed in delight, and Evin grinned. So, they made plans for the boys to spend time together, which they did for the next few cycles. Eventfully, the boys grew apart as they introduced Jon to more responsibilities as a royal son, and Evin took steps to train in the family's import business. They continued to be good friends until Jon went off-world. It had been eight long years since they had seen each other. Now, Jon was again in distress, and Evin, true to his nature, would come to his aid in any way he could.

Evin arrived at the house and quietly told Willem, who answered the door, "Tell Jon we have communicators now. We'll set up a network for reporting, and we also wanted to let him know a group of people have volunteered to help if needed."

Since Jon and Alexis had already gone to bed, Willem reassured him he would give the communicator to the prince in the morning.

CHAPTER 30

"Please state your purpose for traveling to our planet," the young soldier at the counter asked in a bored voice. He barely registered the credentials that both handed over when they had disembarked from the ship.

"We are on a scouting trip for training locations for the Intergalactic Police Academy," Matt answered, in a matching bored voice.

At the mention of the Intergalactic Police, the soldier snapped to attention and looked more closely at them and their documents. "Yes, sir, have a wonderful visit, sir," he stammered, as he handed the papers back.

They moved out of the hanger and into the heat of the day and bright sunlight. Both wanted to go straight to the senator's residence but knew guards would probably follow them, so they moved off toward their hotel first. After renting an air car, they set off to find their lodgings. It was fairly close to the spaceport, which was part of the plan in case they needed to leave. It was a four-story building someone had obviously converted from a former mansion, set back from the road by a long, winding lane. They found the amenities were suitable for an exclusive private hotel. Matt wondered whether they would have time to use any of them.

Their rooms were enormous, and one had a floating bed that seemed a little pompous to Matt. Lu-zan said it was only what they deserved, with a twinkle in his eye. "You can take the bed." He smiled as he went to inspect the other bedroom.

When Lu-zan returned, Matt signaled to check for listening devices. He wanted to be cautious because the government seemed to be very shaky and suspicious. Lu-zan agreed and nodded. They both inspected their rooms using the built-in scanners in their wrist units but found nothing.

They both decided to take a nap first before going out to see a little of the city, not knowing when they would get another chance.

A couple of hours later, refreshed, they left the hotel by air car and traveled to the area closer to the senator's house. There they stopped at a local restaurant and enjoyed a wonderful meal of local vegetables and meat from an animal called a jantelope, a long-legged, deer-like creature with an enormous head. They had a dessert made with thick cream from a local cow-type creature, which the settlers had bought with them when they landed on the planet. Matt patted his stomach, which he felt had grown at least two sizes bigger.

"Let's walk a bit to work off this good food. That was almost as good as Mari's lunch," Lu-zan said, referring to Phillip's wife and the lunch she had made at their campsite. Matt missed the wonderful cooking of his wife. He'd eaten out too many times. He missed home.

Lu-zan looked at his friend and knew what was bothering him. "Don't worry, my friend, you'll be home soon enough and gorging yourself on your beautiful wife's famous chocolate pudding."

"You think so? I hope so," Matt responded.

They wandered along the main street, just looking at the beautiful homes and plentiful businesses, walking past the house twice. Traveling down neighboring lanes and watching the people and the patrols that wound around the area, they checked to see whether anyone was following them, then went back to the air car to move it to another neighborhood close by. After parking the air car on a small side street, they both doubled back to the alley behind the senator's home. They found the small side gate to the home and hoped that Jon and Alexis had arrived unharmed and were waiting for them. After all, they didn't know whether this senator was trustworthy. They only had Jon's memories to judge the man, and men sometimes change, especially under stress.

Matt waited a minute to make sure they were unnoticed, then pressed the button on the gate. They didn't have to wait long. The gate opened and a tall, handsome young man in the uniform of Tariq's military greeted them.

"Mr. O'Shea and Honorable Cinh, please come in."

Matt raised his eyebrow at Lu-zan, who shrugged. They followed the young man into the house where Jon was waiting impatiently and Alexis was holding his hand as if to hold him back from running out to greet them in the garden.

Willem stepped back so Matt and Lu-zan could greet them, and then he invited them into the parlor. Aeneas and his daughter were waiting for them there. They shook hands and felt comfortable in their presence. Anya had a wide smile and stood holding hands with Willem. Alexis smiled at all of them and stood close to Jon.

Matt took charge of the gathering. "I'm Matt O'Shea, and some of you already know Lu-zan. Can we first have an update on what's been happening?"

Senator Aeneas gave everyone a succinct report. He added for Jon's benefit, "Willem's parents, and your brothers and sister, Jon, got to my estate safely. I had my caretaker stock the house before they arrived. They are shielded for now. So now we have to trap Tariq, if we can."

"Jon told me he had an idea on how we could do that, but he won't tell me what it is."

"I have my secrets, but what I want is for you two to remain free agents without endangering Willem's position. I need him in order to get into the palace. Also, I want you to be clear of suspicion so you can enter the palace when I need you."

"You don't ask for much, do you?" Matt scratched his head. "Are you sure it's safe to talk here?"

"We have done a complete sweep for bugs. I think they do additional listening when we report in," the senator informed him.

Jon grinned at him. "You always said not to aim low. Well, I'm aiming for nothing short of General Tariq's complete downfall." His eyes glittered with determination. "That man is engaging in the complete extermination of my family and government, so I intend to exterminate him and his awful plans for our planet instead. I am also worried about the prefect, who is very ambitious, and I doubt Tariq trusts him—at least not completely. After his failure to bring me to the general, he will be doubly dangerous."

Matt asked uneasily, "Is the general, or the prefect, married or have children?" At Jon's pointed look, he defended his question. "I'm just uneasy at the complete destruction of someone with a spouse and/or children. Spouses or children plan for revenge in the future. I just don't wish to get rid of one or two villains only to have to come back to save your butt again in the future."

"No, they are all by themselves, being men who only want power for themselves, so it should be nice and tidy," Jon told him grimly.

"Okay, that's a relief to my sensibilities," Matt replied dryly. "Let's get something to eat while we talk about how we are going to get everyone free of this mess. Senator, can we beg a meal?"

Anya laughed and led them to the kitchen. Lu-zan took her arm and charmed her with jokes. Willem stayed close by, not out of jealousy, but because Lu-zan and his expertise in martial arts fascinated him. He hoped he might get him to show him some useful moves. They might come in handy in this current mess.

In the kitchen, Anya directed Lu-zan and Willem in pulling bottles and jars out of the cabinets, and she grabbed a large roast from the refrigerator. The senator pulled plates and cups from cabinets, and Matt spied napkins on the counter. Together, they soon had a small banquet laid out on the table that included the meat, freshly made bread, olives, and many vegetables. At first, silence reigned as they ate until they were full. Soon, the only one left still eating was Lu-zan.

"Where are you putting it all?" Alexis asked him in amazement. Everyone laughed, including Lu-zan, with his mouth full.

"Lu-zan is famous for the amount of food he can consume. Isn't that right, Jon?" Matt asked.

Jon nodded his head.

"He once had a contest with a huge warrior from the planet, Ceylo. The warrior was twice the size of Lu-zan. The warrior was groaning after ten plates full of food. The man later said he couldn't believe it."

"I think that's a tale," Alexis said, laughing.

"No, no, it's true." Jon held his hand over his heart.

"Oh man, I'm never challenging you," said Willem, rolling his eyes.

Senator Aeneas spoke into the laughter. "I hate to stop the fun, but Willem, Anya, and I have to report into control in a few minutes."

It was a sobering thought and brought the group back to the matter at hand. The group moved back into the parlor, where they arranged themselves on the comfortable furniture. They were all reluctant to break the mood with serious discussion. Matt noticed the beautiful furniture, lovely paintings on the walls, and a portrait of a lovely woman on the mantel. He hoped they could pull this off, so the senator and his family could return to this historical and welcoming home and everyone else on the planet could live in peace.

Willem was the first to break the silence. "We have five minutes before we have to check in, so while we do that, I ask you to stay in here and be silent. It usually only takes a minute, but I like to wait about five minutes afterward to ensure they don't leave the audio open to catch us doing something wrong."

"Okay, I have a plan about how we can do this, but it can wait until you check in to discuss it," Matt suggested.

"Okay."

Willem, Anya, and her father moved into the other room to check in. Everyone else moved away from the door so they couldn't be picked up on the feed. The check-in went fine, but as the senator, Anya, and Willem were returning to the parlor, a knock sounded on the front door. Willem went to see who it was but didn't open the door, as he saw his superior, Sergeant Harper, waiting impatiently on the front porch. Willem glanced back at everyone as he wondered what to do. Matt signaled for him to answer the door as he and Lu-zan moved into positions farther back, out of sight.

"Sergeant Harper, what brings you here?" Willem asked, as he snapped a salute.

"I told you before I would check up on you, Young."

"Yes, sir, you did. We just finished checking in with control. As you can see, the politician and his daughter are right here."

"I think I will stay here, too, and wait for this other royal person to appear," he declared, as he pushed past Willem into the house. "I don't think you should be alone." He rudely eyed Anya as he passed her. She retreated and moved closer to her father, who immediately put an arm around her. Willem was turning red with rage as he stared at his superior.

"I have it under control, I assure you, sir."

"Oh, I think I could be a big help in your vigil." Harper moved closer to Anya and trailed a finger up her arm.

"I would appreciate it, if you would keep your hands to yourself, sergeant!" the senator demanded, as he moved Anya farther away. He could feel Anya fuming in anger next to him.

"I don't think you're able to demand anything, Senator," Harper threatened, his voice dripping with venom.

"Remove your hand. Now," Willem demanded, taking a step closer to him.

"Or what, young man?" Harper said, taunting him.

"Or this," Willem said, as he slugged him. The man went down hard and, unfortunately, struck his head on the edge of the step. He lay on the floor—too silent and too still.

Everyone stared at the silent form, then reality set in as they reacted to the disaster. Matt and Alexis both checked his pulse and shook their heads at Willem and Jon.

"Oh no, is he dead? Oh, Willem," Anya gasped, as she stepped into Willem's arms. He backed away from her and stood with his head bowed.

"I need to turn myself in, I…I have to go." He turned to the group with misery in every movement.

"Wait, let's think this through a moment," the senator murmured. Anya stood calmly as she turned hopeful eyes on her father.

There must be something that we can do, she thought.

"If I turn myself in, how will you get into the palace? I'm sorry I ruined our plans." Willem turned to leave, but Jon gripped his arm.

"We'll think of something. If you admit to killing him, Tariq will kill you."

"There is nothing I can do. It's my duty." Willem turned desolate eyes on Jon. "I'm sorry I let you down, my King."

"I won't let Tariq kill you, my friend. We will find a way out of this mess." Jon turned to all of them. "Think. What was this man like? Willem, would he come alone, or do you think he would tell anyone where he was going, especially since I think he was up to something nefarious."

"I know he often acted alone. He liked to boss everyone around, using his position to get special favors. I didn't see any other soldiers with him when he arrived."

"So, maybe we can assume no one will come looking for him soon," Jon said thoughtfully. "First, let's move him from the hallway so no one can see him through a window or doorway."

Matt and Jon moved the body into the parlor and covered him with a throw from the couch. Then everyone moved to the kitchen to discuss what to do. Anya and her father set out drinks for everyone at the large kitchen table, and they all sat down. They stared at the table as they wrestled with the problem.

"This is not getting us anywhere. Let's revise our plan and come up with something new," Lu-zan stated. "Was this man known for causing trouble?"

Willem nodded and looked up at Lu-zan. Knowledge dawned on his face. "We can use that to our advantage."

Lu-zan nodded agreement. "We just have to figure out how."

"Okay, I think I have a notion about how to do that. Willem needs to get Jon and Alexis to the palace, but Jon admits to killing Harper, so that Willem can apprehend him after the act. We can move the body back to the steps where he initially fell, and that would corroborate Willem's story. Willem will be a hero to Tariq, and you'll be near Tariq. That would increase the trust Tariq has in Willem and might give him more freedom of movement. Willem can tell Tariq that the senator and Anya took advantage of the confusion to run away during the attack. Then I think we need to get them to a secure place. Lu-zan and I can get them to our rooms, where no one would look for them. After we get them to our rooms, Lu-zan and I will go to the palace asking for a public meeting with the king. And they probably will refer us to Tariq. After all, we are on the planet to scout out training locations. Well, what do you think?" Matt looked at each of them. "The only one I don't have an answer for is what Alexis should do. Should she stay with Jon, or should she hide?"

Willem cleared his throat. "We could sneak into the palace by the secret passageways, and she could hide in the royal family's suite of rooms. Leni and Marron told me about some hiding areas she could use. Also, the queen is still hidden there, too. Maybe I can get her into the same area, and she could treat the injuries of the queen. I could take Jon to the general and then 'find' Alexis hiding out."

"How would you explain how she knew the way into the rooms?" Anya looked anxiously from Willem to Alexis.

"Well, she could say that Jon told her about the hiding places and the passageways," Lu-zan supplied.

"Yes, this could work, but Jon, you will be in Tariq's hands. I hope you have a good plan to survive that man."

"There is something important about how the planet works he doesn't know about. That's my main idea. It's the only thing I can think of that will stop him."

"Do you have a chance of coming out of this alive?" Matt asked.

Alexis moved closer to hear Jon's answer.

"I don't know, but it's the only chance we have," Jon answered just as quietly.

"Okay, then let's do this thing," Alexis said, as she took Jon's hand and vowed to herself that Jon would survive this evil man.

"You know the risk you are taking going to the palace."

Jon looked at Willem. "If you don't take me and Alexis, General Tariq will kill you. If we stick to the plan, it should all work out as it should."

"It would be worth it to keep him away from you, Your Highness. You are the hope of our world. I would rather die than let you die."

"Oh, my friend," Jon shook his head, "I am just a man, like you. If something happens to me, my sister and brothers yet live and can carry the fight forward. I just ask that you take care of Alexis and get her clear if you can."

"You two, quit talking like that. This had better work, or I'll kill you myself." Alexis glared at Jon.

He laughed and said, "Yes, ma'am."

The senator stepped up and hugged each of them. "I look forward to seeing you again soon." Anya was steel-eyed as she kissed Willem and told him, "Come back to me soon." When she turned to the others, she hugged each of them fiercely and turned away.

Matt grabbed each of them and told them, "We'll meet you at the palace."

Lu-zan bowed to Alexis. He reminded Willem of the moves he had showed him, and then he turned to Jon. "You are the son of my heart. I am very proud of you and the man you have become. I will see you at the palace." He bowed deeply. Jon returned the bow just as deeply, then stepped forward and gave him a hug.

Willem left with Jon and Alexis in tow to move out of the side garden gate. They moved to the shadowed side of the alley and watched as Matt, Lu-zan, Anya, and the senator exited out of the side gate as well. They waved as they parted in opposite directions.

CHAPTER 31

Matt's group moved cautiously through the alleys until they reached their air car. Anya and her father could hide in the back for the ride to the hotel. Matt kept a close eye out for any patrols, but luckily, they did not see any as they approached the old-style mansion that was the hotel.

"What happens when we get there? I mean, how are we going to get in without being seen?" Anya asked anxiously.

"The hotel rooms on Tyrea don't have landing pads outside each hotel room, so we will stop here and drop you both off. Walk to the back entrance. When I open the door for you, we can then go up together like we are all going to our rooms. Senator, just act like you are looking for your access key if anyone sees you," Matt suggested.

"Lu-zan could go in normally to the restaurant and order something to eat to bring back to the room. He eats so much they won't know he's getting enough food for four. We'll meet him there. Okay?"

"All right. See you shortly." They got out of the air car, then they watched as Matt drove the car around to drop Lu-zan off in front of the hotel before driving around to park it. They walked to the back entrance.

Matt took his time gathering items in the air car in order to give everyone time to get into position. A few minutes later, he left the car and strolled into the hotel. When he thought no one could see him, he hurried to let the senator and Anya into the back entrance. They made their way to the room, where they immediately collapsed.

"Well, I hate to bring this up, but do you think we'll be undetected here?" The senator looked around the room with its two full sized beds. "It's a pleasant room, but hardly big enough for four people."

"Hopefully, we won't be here very long, and I'll put the 'Do Not Disturb' sign on the door. That should keep the maid from cleaning the room. No one should bother you. Willem will have Jon and Alexis at the palace in a couple of hours, and we will settle this mess by late tonight."

Lu-zan came in with a cart full of food. "I suggest we eat this up, and we can put the cart back outside the door."

"Great, I'm starved," everyone said at the same time.

Lu-zan beamed at them like a proud papa as they finished every scrap of food on the cart. "The kitchen didn't believe me when I said I could eat all that. After all, I told them, I have a reputation to keep up." They all laughed at that.

"Anyone want to play a card game? I always carry a pack with me."

A couple of hours later, Matt and Lu-zan left for the palace, leaving the senator to play solitaire and Anya to sleep, each immersed in their own thoughts.

When the air car landed at the palace, they parked in the designated space and announced to the parking attendant that they were there for an audience with the monarch. Admitted to the palace after showing their documents, they walked, escorted, to the king's offices.

"May I help you?" asked a voice issuing from a camera on the desk.

"We have a scheduled audience with the king. I am Matt O'Shea, and this is Lu-zan Cinh, from the Intergalactic Police Training Academy."

"I am sorry, the king is not available. Can I schedule another appointment for you to see the king?" the voice replied. "Or I can refer you to General Tariq's offices."

"We came all this way to see the king. Are you sure he is not available?"

"Yes, if you would like to talk with General Tariq, I can call his office now."

"Of course, thank you, we will wait."

CHAPTER 32

Willem led his little group into the dark and dusty secret passageways of the palace. Jon remembered the fear and excitement he had felt that day, long ago, when he had gotten lost and ended up meeting Evin. Today, he felt the same fear and excitement, but for four different reasons. One, he had to face an insane dictator bent on power. Two, he also felt fear for his world, his family, and his friends, old and new, if he failed in stopping him. Three, he especially felt fear for Alexis, whom he had just found and yet couldn't imagine living without. Four, he felt excitement, as if he were moving toward his predetermined destiny.

"This is like an old horror film with people creeping around in damp, dark tunnels. I'm surprised they still exist after all this time," Alexis whispered in Jon's ear.

"When I was six years old, I ended up out in the alley. Evin, who you met, was eight, found me and brought me home." Jon smiled at the memory.

Willem told her of his experience. "I found the tunnels when I was a child, too, and used to play in them all day while my parents were working."

Jon and Willem shared a brief camaraderie and smiled at their fond memories.

"When you get to the royal apartments, don't forget to check those other hidden passages. I'll be with Jon for a while, but I'll check on you later. You have your medical bag?" Willem nervously asked Alexis.

"Yes, I have it," she assured him.

"Your Highness, I'll wait for your signal to contact Evin on the communicator. Just to verify, you'll use the word, 'friend,' right?"

"Right." Jon could feel his body tensing up. "Alexis, please be very careful as you move around the rooms. The guards might inspect the rooms again."

They arrived at the secret passage into the queen's suite. Jon turned Alexis into his arms and kissed her long and hard. "Steady, I love you."

She touched her lips in surprise and gave him another quick kiss on the cheek before she shouldered her medical bag and turned to go through the opening Willem held for her.

Willem and Jon retreated down several stories to a floor where there was more foot traffic.

"Are you sure you want to do this?"

"It's not a matter of want, but need, and I'm the only one who *can* do it. Let's go. You need to hit me."

"What, why?" said Willem, surprised.

"If you don't, the story you are telling about me killing Harper wouldn't be believed. Make it convincing."

"I'm only doing this because you asked me to," Willem said. He hit Jon hard on the side of his head, splitting the skin and causing the maximum blood flow.

"Does it look convincing?" Jon asked, as he shook his head.

"I hope so, because I'm not doing it again," Willem said.

Willem took his handcuffs out and asked Jon to put his hands behind his back. After Willem had them secured, Jon took a deep breath to steady himself and nodded. Willem cautiously opened the access, and they stepped out into the hallway, where he took Jon's arm and led him toward General Tariq's office. Several other soldiers stood in their way, but Willem stared hard at them and fingered the disruptor rifle he carried. The soldiers grudgingly gave way.

Willem knocked at the door and, at the acknowledgement, marched Jon into the office and wrenched him in front of the general's desk.

"Sir, he came to the senator's house, like you said he would, but Sergeant Harper showed up. There ensued an altercation, and he killed the sergeant. Sir!" Willem reported as he snapped his salute.

General Tariq looked up from some papers on his desk and sat just looking at Jon. "Leave us," he ordered Willem and stood up to confront Jon. "Will you tell me what I want to know?"

"It depends on what you want to know." Jon knew what was going to happen, but it still came as a surprise when Tariq backhanded him across the face. The sharp edges on Tariq's ring tore into Jon's cheek and laid it open to the bone. It immediately formed a white substance and scabbed over, which seemed to fascinate Tariq. Jon, with his hands handcuffed behind his back, could not defend himself. So, Tariq did it again and again and again.

"I just can't tire of doing that," he said with relish. He could see Jon was in a lot of pain as he kept striking him.

Jon blinked the pain away and looked at him with loathing. He could see that Tariq seemed to enjoy seeing the blood and suffering.

"You know I just need you breathing. Not healthy, so I'm going to have some fun first. Your father just didn't last long enough. It was a shame. It would have made things so much easier."

"Murderer!" Jon shouted, as he lunged at him, temporarily overcome by the acknowledgement that Tariq had killed his father. The guards easily restrained him.

"Oh yes, and I enjoyed it. I got the discs from both your father and your mother, though your mother was not as much sport as your father. She seems to have disappeared. Now, I wonder where she could have gone? I don't think she could have gone very far. Do you know where she is, Prince—or sorry, I mean King Jon? I need the code. You know exactly what I'm talking about. Give it to me, and I might spare your life."

He remained silent, so Tariq took a leatherbound stick out of his desk. Jon watched as Tariq walked around him. Jon had time to think it was like being stalked by a very lethal predator, when suddenly the stick struck him across the back of his legs, causing Jon to stumble. He managed to remain silent. Tariq continued to circle Jon, striking before he could brace for the next strike. They grew in strength and speed, causing Jon to work hard to keep on his feet. He could tell that Tariq was getting agitated, and Jon tried to get his breath between strikes. Finally, Tariq threw the stick down on his desk. He turned and looked at Jon, then he smiled a smile so harrowing that it made Jon's blood run cold.

The two guards grabbed Jon and marched him, limping, out of Tariq's office and down the hall toward another room. As he passed Willem, Jon tried to stop, but the guards dragged him past.

"Thanks, friend," he called sarcastically, twisting to look him in the eye. Tariq seemed amused by the comment.

"Friend? What lies did you tell him, I wonder? Never mind, I don't care," Tariq said to Willem.

The guards marched Jon into a room where he could see Tariq did his best work. He hoped Willem remembered the code word because if he didn't, he might die in this terrible room. He looked at the blood spatters on the floor, walls, and ceiling, and wondered whether his father had contributed to the puddles of blood. He looked around and noticed an iron hook hung from the ceiling. Looking at it, the pit in Jon's stomach got even bigger. The soldiers tied his hands in front of him and made him stand on a stool, then raised his hands above his head and caught them over the hook. When they saw he was secure, they kicked the stool away, causing him to fall, with the hook holding his full weight. He grunted with pain.

General Tariq moved to stand in the doorway, leaving Jon in full view for Willem, who stood staring.

General Tariq looked at Willem, seeing the horror in his eyes. "You are dismissed, but I won't forget the service you've done this day. I have room in my new government for innovative young men." He saw the young man blanch at the sight of Jon, bloody and hanging like a piece of meat at the market, and thought he could mold this one.

Willem tore his eyes away from Jon and looked at his commanding officer. "Yes, sir, thank you," he choked out. He turned to leave but stopped short as he saw the prefect coming around the corner.

"Oh, my dear Prefect, you are here. Look at what MY soldier brought me. Too bad you couldn't do as good a job," the general taunted. It gave him such enjoyment to bait him. "Now that you are here, come in and watch as I interrogate him. You might learn something, and I might even let you question him yourself."

Willem stood staring at the door after Tariq and the prefect had gone into the room with Jon. His mind was in a tangle. He wanted to go into that room and rescue the king, yet he knew he couldn't. He wanted to wrench Tariq's and the prefect's hearts out of their chests, but he couldn't do that either. His stomach was churning with disgust at what he had seen. King Jon had given him a mission. He had vowed he wouldn't let him down. He turned and walked away, back toward his room, but as soon as he could, he changed directions, and he ran. Contacting Evin, he urgently relayed the instructions Jon had given him.

CHAPTER 33

Alexis moved into the room that she assumed was the queen's bedchamber, staring first in wonder at the beautiful furnishings, and then she remembered Jon's face as he had talked about his parents and siblings. She touched a small, delicate vase gently, thinking of their peril. *Time to get to work,* she told herself.

She wanted to check all the bolt holes, just in case she needed to get to one quickly. Systematically, she searched the first room she had entered. Willem had told her the locations that Princess Leni had shared with him, so she moved to look at the closest room where the secret passage was through the fireplace. She tugged and pulled and finally slid the false back into the fireplace. She inspected the floor of the passageway to the stairs going down and back. Next, she looked at the chest of drawers Leni had talked about and worked to open it to the passageway, and then she checked the way.

The next bolt hole was in the queen's bedroom, so she cautiously moved into the chambers. Willem had told her where it should be, but she couldn't see any obvious indications of it. She got down on her hands and knees and started in the corner, looking under every piece of furniture and rug. She just couldn't see it, so she got up and started walking around the room, looking at the floor from every angle. It took three circuits of the room before she noticed the slight gap between the floorboards. Following the line of the board, she noticed a similar gap running off at a right angle. She ran her hand along the gap and could feel a slight depression that allowed her to get her fingers under it. Lifting carefully, she opened the bolt hole. It was bigger than she'd thought it would be. After levering her medical bag off her shoulder, she lowered herself down into it and stood inspecting all the space where she was standing, but it surprised her to see it made a turn at one end. Slowly, she moved toward the recessed area. As she got closer, she noticed blood smears. Alexis saw a woman lying on the floor with a torn shoulder slowly seeping blood down her arm.

Alexis knelt next to the woman and felt for a pulse. *Alive, thank God,* she thought. She went back up into the room and grabbed towels, washcloths, and she filled her canteen with water, then returned to the woman. She noticed she had not moved from the position she had found her in. Kneeling, she assembled her tools from her medical bag and the supplies she had grabbed. She started by cleaning the woman's face and removing the cloth from around the wound on her shoulder. The wound was ragged and had done a lot of damage, but it didn't seem deep except in one spot. Alexis sighed in relief that the injury wasn't fatal. She pressed a towel to the wound to slow the bleeding, which caused the woman to groan.

"My Lady, I'm Doctor Alexis Michaels, and I am here to help you. The towel I pressed to your shoulder wound caused the pain you feel. If you are awake, open your eyes now. Come on now, you can do it."

Slowly, the queen opened her eyes and tried to focus. She gasped as she became more aware of the pain. "Water, please."

"Yes, here, drink this. There is more. It's important that you drink as much as you can to ease your dehydration." Alexis carefully gave her a drink from her canteen and placed it close by in case the queen wanted more.

"Let's get this wound cleaned and bandaged, then I'll bring you up-to-date with everything that has happened so far." It didn't take

Alexis long to finish taking care of the shoulder bandaging and get the queen sitting up and leaning against the wall.

"I don't want to move you very far until I have some help, just in case a guard or someone else besides Willem comes into your room to inspect it. There have been a lot of developments, and I'm sure you want to hear about them first."

The queen listened intently to everything Alexis told her. The news that affected her the most was that Jon was here in the palace and had a plan. Alexis worked steadily, applying a fresh bandage and giving her a pressure syringe of painkillers, antibiotics, and a booster to stimulate tissue growth. She wondered to herself about why the queen had not developed the cocoon substance over her wound, but she knew the queen was more interested in news of her family. After telling how Jon had plans to kill Tariq, the queen became very agitated.

"NO, no, please," cried the upset queen. "He'll kill Jon, like he killed my husband."

"He has a plan. Jon has a plan and lots of help. It'll be all right," Alexis insisted, as she tried to calm the queen's fears and her own at the same time. She continued to calm her by telling her about the other children being hidden at Senator Aeneas' country house. She cried, so Alexis shifted away to give her some privacy.

"Thank you for your care," she whispered, as she quieted. She looked around at the dirty area and the deep concern in the lovely eyes of the doctor. She tried to sit up straighter against the wall.

"You're welcome. Are you more comfortable sitting up like that? I need to leave you for a little while. I need to check for my friend, and Your Highness, please drink more water if you can. It will help with your dehydration, and I'll change your bandage in a little while. I have a question, if you don't mind. Why didn't a scab form over your wound? I thought that was a natural response for all people from this planet."

"Oh, no dear. It is a disc only inserted into the shoulders of the royal family. Tariq took mine out of my shoulder so no scab could form and heal my injury."

"That explains a lot, but why didn't Jon know that?"

"That's my fault. I simply didn't think to tell him or the other children about it. We always think there is more time. There were so many things I neglected to tell them," she said sadly.

Alexis squeezed her hand in encouragement and climbed out of the hole. She cautiously leveraged herself out and looked through the rooms for Willem. Her worry for Jon kept rerunning in her brain. His plan seemed insane to her, but Jon kept telling her it was the only way to get close to Tariq. He needed to rely on his natural defenses to protect him long enough to get everyone in place.

A slight scuff sounded just ahead, and Alexis moved to the side wall to inch forward to the corner. A moment later, Willem's head peeked around the edge. Just in time to catch her as she sagged in relief.

"Whoa, are you okay?" Willem whispered.

Alexis blushed and moved away from his supporting arms.

"Just embarrassed," she said. "I found her. She's alive but can't stand. Can you help me get her moved?" She led the way, and they hurried into the recessed area. The queen started in fear when she saw Willem's uniform in the dim light.

"It's okay, Your Highness, it's me, Willem."

The queen eyed the uniform and then looked at him. She knew this man. Then realization dawned. "You're Suri and Gregory's son, aren't you? I'm sorry I can't seem to remember much from when you helped me."

"I helped you get into the bolt hole. Let me help you again."

The queen nodded agreement.

Between Alexis and Willem, they got her up and out. Willem carried her to a nearby chair. Alexis went back to grab her medical bag, canteen, and clean up the bloody mess. Willem kneeled next to the queen, telling her again about the children and assuring her that they were safe. He pulled out his communicator and contacted Evin. The queen listened as Willem told Evin about finding her and how they needed to find a way to move her somewhere safer. When he got done, he smiled at her, as he said that there was another doctor coming, too.

"Why, Alexis is here?" the queen asked.

"Oh, that's splendid news." Alexis had worried about the queen's medical condition, and she would not be there to help. "You're still dehydrated, Your Highness. Please keep drinking the water. I gave you a painkiller, so it should soon feel better. Willem and I both have an important part to play in Jon's plan, so I'm going to be turning over your care to another doctor. I don't know his or her name, but I'm sure the people who love you have picked only the best." Alexis smiled.

"Don't you think it's time you call me Lenore, Alexis?" The queen looked at her in gratitude. She closed her eyes and rested against the back of the chair. She was bloody, dirty, and a little smelly, but Alexis thought this woman had an aura about her that said she would survive. It was that attitude that had saved her life and given her the courage to crawl into the bolt hole after the attack. How she admired that strength and hoped she would have the same strength when she needed it.

Distracted, it surprised Alexis when the chest of drawers opened and emitted four men and one woman who carried a medical bag. She had forgotten the secret passageway but was relieved to get the queen to better shelter. She brought the doctor up-to-date on the care she had given the queen and the injections she had administered to ease her pain and battle any infection that she might have contracted lying on the dirty floor of the bolt hole.

"Hey, I made that chair!" one man whispered, as they looked at the beautiful furnishings. Some men recognized pieces they had made as well. It made them proud that the king and queen valued their work.

"In here, hurry," Willem called, and the men hurried with their tools into the next room. They were shocked and angered to find the queen in such poor condition. They braced the chair while the doctor conferred with Alexis and ended up applying an additional compress to the wound to protect it during the move. Willem opened the false fireplace back for them to use. It was larger, and the chair would fit through easily. Alexis said her goodbyes to the queen and wished her a speedy recovery. It surprised her she felt so close and responsible for this woman in such a short time.

Willem gestured that they also move through the fireplace opening. Together, they moved down two floors, but before they got to the hidden entrance, he stopped her.

"I need to prepare you for what you are going to see at the general's office. Jon was in terrible shape when he gave me the code word for calling for help. Brace yourself."

He led her through a small door. He cautioned her to silence, and they tiptoed to the end of the hall. "Let's go," he whispered, as he took her arm. The guards snapped to alert and then they stared suspiciously at Willem, who didn't give them time to speak. The guards muttered among themselves. Willem pulled his disruptor and looked at each one.

"Just try it. Now where is the general? He will want to talk to this woman."

"Who are you to say what the general will want to do?" demanded one guard. The others murmured agreement, eyeing Alexis up and down, and some of them moved closer.

"Fine, we'll wait, but I wouldn't wish to be you when he finds out you let her stand out here instead of telling him she was here. The skin left on your body won't cover a fly." Willem held onto Alexis' arm and pulled her closer as he leaned back against the wall like he was ready to wait forever.

The guards looked at each other uneasily. After all, they had seen what the general could do to a person. Finally, the senior officer broke down and knocked on the door of the torture room. He looked at Willem and Alexis while they waited.

The door slammed open, and the general stormed out. Blood covered him, and he was obviously furious that anyone would disturb his session of torture. From the room itself came a low moan. Alexis was startled when she recognized the voice. Willem tightened his grip on her arm. The slight movement drew Tariq's attention to them, and he turbulently stormed over to Willem.

"What is the meaning of this interruption?" he demanded.

The prefect meandered out of the room, but his demeanor changed when he saw Alexis. She glared at him.

Willem forcibly drew Alexis forward. "I found her on level eight, wandering around. I thought you would want her here, sir." Willem snapped to attention and pushed Alexis forward.

"Who is she?"

"She says she's Prince Jon's girlfriend. She was trying to find him."

The prefect added from the doorway, "She was the doctor on the prison planet who was treating Jon. She must have helped him escape."

"Is she now? Well, you found him," he said to her. "Let's show you your boyfriend now. Maybe you'll want a real man instead." He stroked his bloody hand down her cheek. "Bring her," he told Willem, his tone of voice turning mean.

Willem took a firm hold on her arm and followed him back into the torture room. Willem whispered to Alexis, "Courage."

Alexis steeled herself for what she might see, but nothing prepared her for the sight of Jon as he hung by his wrists. Stripped to the waist and beaten all over. The webbing covered some injuries in white patches, but even they were bloody. Beaten so fast and hard, the protection from his disc had no time to repair him between blows. Jon was semi-conscious and jolted awake when Tariq threw water on him.

"Maybe you can get him to give me the code," he told Alexis.

She looked at this monster in a man's skin and wrested out of Willem's grip so fast he lost his hold on her. She sprang at Tariq, trying to claw his eyes out, leaving long, bloody streaks running down his chin. Tears ran down her cheeks even as Willem tried to get control of her again.

"Let me go, let me kill him," she screamed.

The prefect backhanded her so hard she fell to the floor, bloody with her cheek flayed open. "Oh my, this could be helpful." He looked at Tariq, who was straightening his clothes. "Yes indeed, don't you agree, General?"

Tariq looked at Alexis and then at Jon. "Mmm, what do you think, Jon?"

Jon moaned and said, "No, no, no. Leave her alone, she doesn't know the code."

"Oh, I think yes, yes, yes. Bring her," he said to Willem, and he ordered the other guards to drag Jon behind him, a gruesome parade down the hallways. Willem followed them, still holding Alexis.

CHAPTER 34

General Tariq looked in triumph at Jon as he lay at his feet in the ancient antechamber. Jon couldn't seem to get to his feet to move toward the transporter. The uneasy guards had just let him drop and now stood around watching the general. The prefect watched from the corner of the small room, wondering whether he would learn anything he could use against the general when he made his own move for power.

Tariq kicked Jon to get him to move toward the platform. "Get up there. You, too, my dear," he said, smiling as he gestured toward Alexis. Alexis leaned down to help Jon get onto the transporter platform. The general took a gun from a guard, and he and the prefect joined them.

When the transporter stopped, it amazed Alexis as she looked around at the gleaming and spotless room that contained a large, low table that would hold one person, a bank of controls, and a keypad.

"Get up on the table, my dear. This shouldn't hurt unless Jon makes a mistake." Tariq laughed and gestured with his gun.

"No," she said, and crossed her arms.

The prefect moved to backhand her again, but Tariq stopped him with a glance.

"No? I don't think you understand." He pivoted and hit Jon hard across the face with his gun. Jon staggered back from the blow and would have fallen if Alexis hadn't caught him.

"Oh, I enjoy that. I could do that all day." He smiled at the prefect, who looked uneasy. "Get on the table now," he told her again, as he pointed to the low table in front of an enormous machine.

Alexis looked helplessly at Jon, who gave her a brief nod and a little smile to encourage her. The table itself surprised her because it wasn't uncomfortable, it just seemed to warm and conform to her shape and size.

"Now, Jon, enter the code. You remember it now, don't you?" Tariq taunted.

Jon limped over to the keyboard and slowly entered a code. Alexis held her breath, not knowing what to expect. Alexis felt a pleasant warmth and a small prick in her shoulder, but other than that, nothing more. She looked over at Jon, who wasn't looking at her, but she noticed Tariq was watching Jon closely, and Jon seemed to be watching the controls.

"That's fine, my dear. You can get down now. Now…" Tariq said, as he pointed his gun at Jon. Alexis fell off the platform, drawing his attention. It was the chance Jon had been waiting for as he swept his leg around and under Tariq, knocking his legs out from under him and slamming him into the prefect. Alexis ran to Jon, but he yelled, "Get on the transporter!" He ran, being careful to keep himself between Tariq and Alexis. Just as he got to the transport platform, Tariq fired, hitting Jon in the back.

"No," Alexis screamed, as Jon fell into her arms. They dematerialized out of the room.

Tariq stared at the transporter, consumed with rage that his prey had gotten away. He turned to the prefect, demanding, "Go after them, you idiot," shoving him toward the transporter. He wanted to tear the place apart, but there was nothing in the room except the machine. A machine he desperately needed. After a few moments, he got himself under control and turned toward his destiny. He walked to the table and climbed onto it to lie down. Looking around one last time, he turned to the keyboard and typed in the code Jon had used. "Don't want to make a mistake, now do we," he said to himself, as he pushed the button.

CHAPTER 35

Jon and Alexis re-appeared in the transporter room with Alexis staggering under Jon's weight. She couldn't see anything except Jon as she fought to stop the bleeding. The prefect materialized on the transporter next and saw Matt and others coming forward to help her and Jon. He took advantage of the confusion to slip from the room. No one noticed his departure. Matt had to bodily move Alexis aside so another doctor could bend to examine her for injuries. She fought to get back to Jon, but another doctor was already assuring her she would deal with Jon's many wounds. She could see the white substance was already forming over the wound in his back.

"Let me go, I'm a doctor, I have to help him," she cried, as she fought Matt's hold.

"Alexis, it's me, Matt O'Shea. The doctors you met earlier are here and will take care of Jon until you can, I promise. It's all right now. We need to take care of your injuries first. You have a nasty cut on your cheek. It needs medical attention, too."

Matt passed her to Lu-zan, who removed her from the room, following the gurney carrying Jon away. Then he motioned to Willem to go with her and Jon.

When Lu-zan returned, he and Matt moved to go through the transporter. At Matt's signal, they arranged themselves to cover the maximum room when they materialized. As they stepped down into the chamber, they met their first surprise. The chamber was empty.

"Where did he go?" Matt asked the empty air. They conducted a thorough search, tapping walls and looking for hidden panels or doorways. Matt then walked over to the machine and thought he saw the answer there, but he would need to talk to Jon for confirmation. If Jon lived through his injuries.

"Let's go see Jon and Alexis, if she ever lets us near either of them again," Lu-zan spoke from behind him.

Matt turned to look at him. "Yes, let's go."

Matt and Lu-zan were both impatient to talk with Jon, but first, that meant they needed permission from Dr. Alexis Michaels, and that was not a simple matter, as she had become very protective of her patient. Finally, she announced they could have a few moments alone with him.

They entered the room to find Jon holding Alexis' hand as he lay on the bed. He looked like hell, but his eyes were bright, clear, and fixed on Alexis.

"I guess I'm going to need another survival specialist again," Matt said with a grin. Jon just returned the grin. "I have another question. What happened to Tariq and the prefect when you left that chamber?"

Jon's grin widened into a smile. "Tariq almost had it, but what he didn't know was the machine recognized a new code only once. Each of our codes is unique, so if he entered the same code I used for Alexis, the machine would read it as a threat. It would have simply removed the threat. Did anyone see the prefect leave the chamber?"

"No, the chaos in the transporter room must have allowed him to escape. We'll look for him," Lu-zan assured him, when he saw Jon's expression turn serious.

Jon's eyes widened, and he surprised everyone when he made the unexpected urgent announcement and struggled to rise. "I have to get to the audience chamber. Now!"

"You can't, you're too hurt," Alexis protested.

"You don't understand, I have to complete the link."

"I thought the link existed already. I don't understand what more you need to do?"

"Please, there is no time now to explain. Come and watch," Jon said through clenched teeth. "Please hurry."

Lu-zan and Matt exchanged glances and moved to order everyone to the audience chamber. The confused regular guards and doctors all surrounded Jon's gurney to wheel him that way. There were many people already in the chamber, and the regular guards were ushering the crowd out when Jon stopped them.

"They need to see this link happen."

Matt looked around the room, automatically taking in any threats, the various entrances, and the large, triangular shape behind the throne chairs. He noted that the color of the palace guard uniforms were a different color than the one wore by Willem, so he divided his men and the palace guards between watching the doors and watching the crowd for any signs of trouble. He hurried back in time to see Lu-zan trying to help Jon stand.

"Wait, do you need to stand? Can't you just do what you have to do lying down?"

"No," Jon replied. "Help me get to the Poeirlinum."

"The what…in um?"

"Up there to the triangle thing."

"Oh, okay, here we go," and he picked Jon up and carried him up the steps. "Now what?"

"Get my clothes off of me. I need to align my spine with the chair."

"Now? Here, in front of all these people?"

"Yes, do it now. Hurry, please."

Lu-zan followed Jon's orders, not understanding why his friend had become an exhibitionist. Alexis moved to block the public's view as much as possible.

Jon stepped back and lay against the triangle interface.

As the minutes passed, everyone retreated down the steps to stand together. The Poeirlinum glowed brighter and brighter, and Jon changed. Alexis gasped and stretched out her hand toward him.

Her cry caused Jon to open his silver eyes and focus on her. He wondered whether she would stay with him after he became what he would become.

The Poeirlinum became even brighter, so bright it was harder and harder to see. He heard gasps from the crowd of people, and then everything faded from his view.

Jon appeared to sink into the triangle. The ridges along his spine opened and fit into the grooves behind him, and the projections, or horns, as Jon thought of them, slid into the two grooves positioned behind his head. Tiny electrodes were imbedded by the Poeirlinum into his spinal column, and nanobots poured into his system. The procedure was not painless, and Jon panted as he fought for control while the machine worked its wonders on his body. He had some idea of what was happening, because he had been standing where Alexis and his friends were standing now when his father transformed. He thought sadly, *I never imagined that I would have to endure the same pain this soon. My father should have lived a long life.*

He remembered holding his mother's hand as his father cried out and how it had shaken them with emotion, but he also remembered the joy when it was over and his father had returned to them. Changed, but still the same. Physically, his father had lost his hair and had subtle protrusions on his head. His spine now had ridges down its length, but he'd let Jon run his hands over the horns and down the ridges, and he'd talked to him about what had happened. Mentally, he was still his father, and he later explained that the machine changed him in order to communicate easily with him.

The planet took from Jon's body information it needed, as it had from his father and his father before him, and in return it showed him how to communicate with it about the people's requests for cleaning the water supply, moving needed resources for both human and animal, and how to maintain air quality and circulation. The machine also imparted to him its greatest secret. It was an artificial entity, created by a race of beings, long vanished from this realm of space. The race of beings was called the Grasteners, which was the closest the planet could get the name so Jon would understand. It played a history for Jon, which it revealed as if Jon were living it himself. He learned the Grasteners created a world that they could interact with easily. A picture appeared in his mind of a race of beings that were vaguely humanoid, with a ridged spine and horns on their heads.

But he mentally protested, *I'm not descended from Grasteners. Why do I have the same features?*

The answer appeared in the shape of a memory, as it gave each royal child the potential for the ridged spines and horns when presented to the machine and implanted with the disc. The disc also gave them protection against injury. This was a precaution, in case the planet needed to call for service—at least one royal could serve if needed. If the planet didn't need someone, the features and the disc would remain dormant. The planet continued its story, as Jon saw the building of the world and how it worked. He saw the Grasteners design the systems within the world and why they connected the running to themselves, with one representing all. The Grasteners were a peaceful race, and lived in their world for millions of years, but they found they were gradually dying out with fewer and fewer children being born. Thousands of years ago, the last Grasteners died, and the planet was alone.

He saw the planet had remained alone until one day humans crashed onto its surface. It had waited patiently, learning about the unfamiliar presence it detected. Jon could feel the impatience building to do something, as the planet felt its systems slowly decay. It didn't know about dying, but it knew that one day all its systems would cease to work, and it would no longer exist. Over time, it learned enough about the settlers to realize that they meant no harm to it. Rather, they tried to repair the damage that was taking place. It judged it was time it made itself known.

The planet picked a warm evening and lifted a platform up out of the ground near one settlement. Then it tried to make appealing sounds. This was a novel experience for it, and the sounds that it issued were harsh and discordant to the settlers. They rushed to see what was making the unusual noises. They tried to be cautious, not knowing whether some new animals had roamed into their area. A few were braver than the others and arrived at the platform first. Jon could see them in his mind and wondered whether one of them was his ancestor. The answer came.

"Yes, this one." The view shifted to show a man, one of the first to arrive. He stood tall, even taller than the other settlers, but he was careful not to get too close to the platform.

"Hello?" he called out, looking around.

"What, you think it will answer you?" one man scoffed at him.

"Touch me and you will understand," came the booming voice. The entire group fell back in astonishment.

Against the quiet hush that fell, and the sudden quiet of the surrounding glade, the first human spoke.

"Who are…what are you?"

"I am the keeper," the machine said, trying to find words the settlers would understand. It had tried to download their language so it could communicate. "I keep the world."

"What do you mean, you keep the world?" the human demanded.

"Touch me, and you will know," the machine answered. This demand set off a wild discussion among all the humans. By this time, the other settlers had arrived, and a huge argument was starting. The machine tried to follow, but the words were indistinct.

"Touch me, and you will understand," it repeated in its loud voice.

"Why?" asked the one who would be his ancestor.

"It is the way I am made," came the answer.

Hesitantly, the man approached with an outstretched hand.

"What are you doing?" a few settlers shouted at him, and a few tried to catch his arm, so he stopped and looked back at them.

"We'll never know unless someone touches it." And with that, he touched the cool surface of the platform. He immediately found himself immersed in the machine's memories and gripped in its desperate need.

CHAPTER 36

Evin and his loyal companions filed into the audience chamber. They saw the new king pinned to the fixture behind the throne chairs and the group down the steps from it. They looked around and could see various soldiers milling around, glancing uneasily up to the front of the hall.

After the townspeople got the call from Evin to move into the palace, he told the various groups to disburse to different portions of the palace. Some he directed into the cells below, hoping to find the missing ministers and other prisoners, like family members being held as hostages. A remarkable number of released people were told to go to the Audience Hall as witnesses for what was to come. It had been a very long time since a king had melded with the Poeirlinum. The last time anyone remembered was when Jon's father had accepted the position. Some protested because they were dirty and smelled, but the importance of this moment convinced them.

Evin looked around and could see the now scattered ministers in the crowd. As the crowd saw them come in, there was a murmur that was growing louder the longer the crowd waited.

As his men and women returned, Evin signaled to several who then disbursed throughout the hall, coming to stand behind any soldiers. Now all they had to do was wait for any sign of trouble.

Willem saw him first; a slight movement behind a pillar caught his attention. When he looked more closely at the pillar, he could see part of the prefect's profile. He was staring up at Jon, and Willem noticed he had something in his hand. Willem wasn't sure what threat this represented, so he signaled to Lu-zan, and they moved to where they could talk undisturbed but remain watchful. Willem explained the situation, and Lu-zan nodded understanding and started moving around the hall toward the prefect's position.

Willem signaled to Evin, and they met at the back of the hall. Willem again explained about seeing the prefect, and they agreed to come at him from opposite directions to cut off any escape. Willem thought of the movement as a tense dance. Groups of citizen volunteers were shadowing soldiers, and a group comprising himself, Lu-zan, and Evin were converging on the prefect.

The prefect began moving, and it soon became evident he was maneuvering to get into a better position. He angled behind a pillar closer to the stage, and everyone felt an urgent need to get closer. It was apparent as the group grew ever closer that he still seemed to have something in his hand.

Lu-zan was almost there, and he could see it was a gun in the prefect's hand. He watched as the prefect moved once more to the next pillar, ever closer. There he paused and brought his hand up, sighting along the barrel. Lu-zan could tell by the angle he was aiming at Jon as he laid defenseless on the Poeirlinum.

Lu-zan gathered himself and, without hesitation, launched himself across the remaining space between him and the prefect. He slammed into the man just as he fired at Jon, causing it to tear into Lu-zan, and the beam from the Poeirlinum enveloped Lu-zan in a protected cocoon of white. The rest of the group arrived just as Lu-zan's cocooned body fell on the floor in front of the prefect. The unexpected result caused the prefect to hesitate to aim again.

Evin was closest and took advantage of the prefect's confusion to approach, when suddenly a stroke of white lightning again shot out from the Poeirlinum to the prefect. When it died away, the prefect was unconscious on the floor.

Matt hurried over to check that he was still alive.

"Well, that takes care of him. It will relieve Jon that he won't have to hunt him down."

A commotion sounded behind him, and he turned to find that several soldiers were now trying to bolt from the room. The ministers, men and women, who had been in the cells until recently, were not gentle with them. Matt imagined the soldiers were the ones who had taken part in the incarceration of the ministers. They probably thought the Poeirlinum would reach out for them, too.

You know, Matt thought, *maybe that would be interesting.* He smiled, despite being a peaceful man at heart.

Willem looked around at all the people crowded in the hall. Some, mostly the ministers, were angry and looking to take out that frustration on the general's soldiers, who had abused them. The guards who had been identified so far as being part of the general's squadron were being marched out of the hall by Evin's men.

Willem saw a movement at the foot of the steps near the throne chairs. He looked closer and recognized the soldier who often had taken the most enjoyment in handing out punishments. Most people in the hall wouldn't know who he was because he had taken his uniform coat off and torn the pinstripe off the side of his trousers. Willem shouted to Matt, "Stop him," pointing the soldier out to the other man.

The soldier panicked at being discovered, and rushed at Alexis, knocking her back into Matt, pushing both of them off their feet. Matt struggled to regain his stance but saw he would be too late. The soldier climbed the steps toward Jon, and Matt despaired that no one was between them. Jon was unaware of his danger. From the far side, Willem came running and launched himself across ten feet to clip the soldier right across the back of his limbs. The soldier went down hard, rolling with the fall and trying to dislodge Willem from his hold. Willem held on, and soon more people all piled on to pin the soldier to the floor. The ministers were kicking and biting the man, and sometimes doing the same to Willem, seeing only the dreaded uniform.

Alexis waded into the fray to protect Willem by yelling, "Not him, he's one of the good guys." Willem separated himself from the entanglement of limbs.

"Lucky that soldier didn't pull a knife on anyone. Oh, oh, I spoke too soon," Matt said, looking down at Willem's stomach.

"What?" Willem looked at Matt, then he felt it, the burn of a knife slash. "Damn," was all he got out before his legs gave way. Matt caught him on his way down.

"Alexis," Matt yelled, "Willem's hurt."

Alexis joined the group at Willem's side. "Jon's going to be upset that he missed all the fun. Let me look at it," she told Willem, as he watched Alexis raise his shirt to examine him.

"Oh, I think it's just a flesh wound," Willem said stoically.

"I hope so because I think there is going to be a party to celebrate, and I wouldn't want you to miss it because you're in a hospital," Matt teased him.

"I will not miss any party. No way, no how." He let the other guards take him to be tended, still protesting that he would not miss any party, which made everyone smile.

Matt commented to the group, "Now all we have to do is wait for Jon and Lu-zan to come back to us. I think Evin and Willem can send word for everyone to come back to the palace. Jon will want his family here, and I know Anya will want to see Willem. We have a lot of work to do getting ready to welcome the new king."

Smiling, everyone whispered, and Matt turned to retrieve the prefect, only to find he had escaped in all the excitement.

"We need to mount a search for the prefect, after all. He's gone."

Everyone turned, startled, to look at the spot where he had lain unconscious moments before, and at his guard, rubbing his sore head. Evin looked disgusted and turned to his friends. "Looks like we still have work to do. Let's get started looking for him. We don't want him to spoil our party." He led the way out of the room.

"I think we should let them do it. We need to stick close to Jon and should be here for Alexis, as soon as she returns from dealing with Willem," Matt suggested to a nearby soldier, who agreed. "Maybe that beam did something to the prefect, and they will find him in the hallway melted into a puddle."

"We should be so lucky," the soldier muttered.

CHAPTER 37

That brave soul from Jon's vision was one of his many times removed ancestors. Throughout the years, other ancestors served. The artificial intelligence called Tyrea showed Jon the many wonders that the creators built into its structure. He saw marvels like the many waterfalls, which aerated the water and provided the atmosphere with moisture. It showed him the closed water system that kept a certain volume of water, so there was always plenty for the future. Jon saw how the internal workings of the planet provided for the needs of its surface dwellers. It showed him the recent history of humankind on the planet, and how his ancestors had protected the planet in return. It promised to show him more every time he made contact. Last, it showed him his father, and shared how much the planet mourned him. Tears came to Jon's eyes as he felt the planet's sorrow echo his own.

"I'm glad and grateful." Jon fell silent. He was so overwhelmed by the information the planet had given him.

The planet had analyzed Jon's physical condition as it placed its probes. It found and repaired the damage by the gun, and other many injuries. Jon could feel the repairs and the immense relief imparted by the machine. He could read and analyze parts of the machine so that they became truly linked. Jon learned how he could open his mind to let him know about the well-being of the planet. He did so now and directed the machine to different parts of the world where attention was needed and where quakes, at this very moment, were threatening its overall integrity. He directed the air circulators to repair the depleted ozone layer for protection until it was back into balance. He tiredly asked one last question of the machine, a question that caught the planet by surprise.

"Are you sentient?"

"What is sentient? I know my systems, I breathe, I circulate the air and water, I need to create, I communicate. Is that sentient? I am aware, so I think, yes, I am sentient."

"Good enough." Jon opened his eyes and let them roam all around the room. It startled him to see the cocoon lying next to the Poeirlinum.

Who is in the cocoon? he mentally asked the machine.

The machine sent back images to Jon about what had happened.

Is he alive? Will he heal? Jon asked.

"Yes, he is mending well, and the cocoon should open soon," the machine sent.

Jon relaxed in relief.

Jon looked around the room and marveled at how far the human settlers had come with their planetary ally. The room was beautiful, and now that he knew its accurate history, he understood some of the symbology used on the columns and arches. He could see what looked like technical apparatus and tiny humans interacting to build a road or a bridge. It was wonderful. His eyes wandered down to the thrones. His heart warmed at what he saw there. Alexis was asleep in one of the throne chairs with clothes draped over the arm.

The audience chamber was almost empty. He wondered how long since he had lain back against the metal. He stepped down from the slab and lost his balance. Exhausted, he found he was very feeble and starving.

The slight noise he had made awakened Alexis. She blinked up at him, almost falling when she tried to get out of the chair, fighting her way through the clothes. Jon was just in time to catch her. They supported each other as they stood there staring. She let her hands explore him, marveling at the new, smooth skin with no sign of damage from the gun or whip.

"What happened to you?" she whispered to him.

"The Poeirlinum happened to me. There is so much to tell you. But first, will you marry me?" Jon asked in a rush, afraid she might refuse him after all that had happened.

"No…I, I don't know. After all, a girl doesn't want to rush into anything like marriage," she joked, but couldn't continue when she looked at his beloved face. "Let's talk about that later."

"Okay," he replied in disappointment. A loud grumble sounded from his stomach as it protested the long absence of food. "Let's go eat," he said.

"Wait, a minute there. You need some clothes, and this." She grabbed his hand and turned him back to her, then took his head into her hands to kiss him. The kiss deepened, and Jon hugged her to him.

CHAPTER 38

A mysterious visitor appeared in Jon's chambers the day after Jon had undergone the session on the Poeirlinum. Jon started to call for the guard when the figure called softly.

"My King, Jon, don't you recognize me?"

The voice was familiar to Jon. The man appeared foppish but also familiar to him. He looked closer. The voice was similar, and the height was the same, and then Jon noticed the eyes with their twinkle.

"Z? Is that you?"

"Yes indeed, cousin." He removed his wig. "At your service, my King," he added, as he knelt to Jon.

"None of that between us. Get up. Tell me why you are here and dressed like that. Are the rest of the family okay?" After seeing the treatment of the ministers and their families in the capital city, he berated himself for not thinking of the ministers and families on the other continents.

Z looked at his cousin and told him, "We have been very concerned about the recent developments in the capital city of the military alliance, and it has turned out to be justified."

"But, why the disguise?"

"That was Mother's idea. She and Father have built the outfit over the years by adding padding, so I looked like I had put on weight. She also helped me with the mannerisms so I would appear coyer when needed. I tell you I'm really tired of it, but in times such as these, it is very necessary."

"Hopefully, you will soon be able to go without it, but why are you here?"

"I have been following Minister Wayne and gathering information on what Tariq was trying to do. I had a man working in Tariq's guards sending me information, but he hasn't responded recently, and I fear he is dead. Tariq was always violent, but now he's revealed himself as also deranged. I am glad he is dead, but I know you suffered under his hand. I'm sorry I couldn't help save your father. He was a good king to the people and a wonderful uncle. I will miss him."

"Thank you, Z."

"Watch out for Minister Wayne. I don't know how much he knows about what has happened here. He might not realize that Tariq is dead, or even if the king is dead. I think he will try to do some mischief in the future."

"I'm still glad to see you, disguised or not. Hopefully, we can talk again later."

"I am ever at your command, my King," Z answered with a bow and a smile.

CHAPTER 39

They draped the palace in black for four weeks in memory of King Borig and those who had lost their lives during General Tariq's insane campaign for power. The people had loved their king and knew he had died a brave death defending their world. Tariq had killed senators, business people, soldiers, men, women, and children while in power. Statues and tributes would take place after the ceremony of passage of rule.

After the four-week period of mourning took place, Jon felt the people needed something good to remember. The planet could take as long as necessary to mourn the loss of his father and the others, but right now, people needed to be reassured of their security and to laugh and appreciate the living.

Everyone who had fled now returned to the city. The queen had a tearful and joyful reunion with all of her children and her nephew, Z, who stayed to keep watch for Minister Wayne. They mourned in private for their father and uncle. Willem greeted his parents and the royal children. The politician and Anya came home to the loving embrace of all. Everyone was very careful of the care of the queen because she had just had a session with the Poeirlinum to heal her wounds and replace her disc, and she was still a little sore and tired. The senator and Anya came and joined with Willem and his family.

The queen and the senator spent a lot of time together, but Jon knew they were his father's best friends, so he left them at peace to mourn. Joy overcame the ministers at being reunited with their families and friends.

Everyone in the palace spent the days of mourning cooking and cleaning. There were a lot of smiles and laughter, and rumors ran rampant about the new king and his lady love as life returned to normal.

A few important details still had to be taken care of. The spies that had been up on the space station and Tariq's soldiers were in custody. All were awaiting judgment from the planetary court. The only one not accounted for was the prefect, who was still at large. Everyone was on the lookout, but they wouldn't allow it to cast a shadow over the party.

Jon had not pressed Alexis about marriage, but she knew she would need to give him an answer. The days of mourning were long ones for Alexis. She withdrew from almost everyone and spent her time in her quarters thinking of her choices. The displayed hologram of her lost love was on her shelf, and she spent a lot of time talking to it. Being a practical woman, she made lists of pros and cons. She wrote letters of rejection and acceptance to Jon, not knowing which one she would use.

"Okay, what if I return to the prison hospital, what then?" she asked out loud, repeatedly. She instinctively knew that part of her life was over. She missed the life and friends she had there, but she felt she couldn't return to it.

Back and forth, she argued, but it came down to one question. *Do you love him?* she asked herself.

The hologram seemed to speak to her. *If you love him, don't lose him. What we had was beautiful, but you need to get on with your life. Besides, he needs you, and you need him.*

Finally, she had some clarity.

The day of rejoicing arrived.

First on the agenda was the acceptance of the king. Jon felt a range of emotions as he stood with head bowed in gratefulness, sadness, and love. Other emotions also flowed through his mind, like friendship and wonder. He raised his head and repeated the ancient words.

"I, Jon Tor, promise to commit my life to the preservation of the entity called Tyrea. Also, I promise to strive for the advancement, protection, and care of all life on the planet. So say I this day."

Thunderous applause greeted him.

Jon and Alexis started the festivities with acknowledgements. Jon first turned to acknowledge all those who had played a big part in getting him home and to this point. Second, he asked the imprisoned ministers and their families to come forward. They had borne the blunt of Tariq's sadomasochism and suffered in the palace dungeons. To them he gave each a Roseate of Bravery and compensation for the loss they'd suffered. He also told them, "I will record your names in the records to remember forever your contributions to freedom." He shared the names of those who had died at Tariq's hand and had no living families to carry on their memories.

"I can't return the lives lost, but we all share your sorrow. I can only promise to never forget their help and yours in securing our future. May we always remember what happened here. Thank you all."

He then called Evin and his volunteers. "Evin, you have ever been my friend, and I am eternally grateful. You and your team will receive monetary rewards for the goods lost in this struggle, but also, I want to appoint you as the City Guard to be called on for special duties. I can't thank you enough for all the new friends made and for the bravery shown. Thank you with all my heart, my friends. And one last thing," Jon continued, smiling. "Evin, it is my sincere wish that you would accept the position of Commander of the City Guard."

Evin accepted while his entire team cheered.

Jon called Willem out next, but a commotion had started at the door. A loud voice demanded entry. Everyone turned to stare at who had interrupted the proceedings.

"Why are all these people here?" the man demanded, as he looked around the hall.

"Minister Wayne, how nice of you to come for our celebration. How can we help you?"

"I came to see General Tariq. Where is he?"

"Well, I don't know for sure, but he no longer works here." Several people sniggered softly.

"And who are you?" the minister asked.

"My manners are lacking, I apologize. My name is Jon Tor, and I am the new king of Tyrea." He bowed. "How may I help you?"

"You can't. It is too bad your father is dead. Now there was a man worthy of conversation."

Jon stiffened. "Perhaps we should talk in private?"

Marron pushed forward, but the queen caught his arm.

"Minister Wayne, your General Tariq is dead by his own hand after he killed my husband, tortured my sons and me, threatened my daughter, and mistreated and killed our friends. If you can behave, you may stay, but if not, I can offer you a very personal tour of our dungeons. Which will it be?"

He glanced around at all the hostile faces. "Perhaps I need an attitude change. My apologies, my King and Queen Mother. I'll stay."

Willem stood at attention with his arm strapped to his side because of his injury. Suri and Gregory smiled at their son as Jon gave the promotion of Captain of the Royal Guard to the young man. He would be responsible for the protection of the royal family. Anya took the senator's hand and held on tight as she beamed at her love. Willem looked over at her and the senator and noticed Marron and Vrai grinning at him from the dais. He grinned back.

Next called were Senator Aeneas and Anya. Jon had a hard time coming up with an appropriate acknowledgement for the senator or for Anya. They had both lived a nightmare of uncertainty in order to provide Jon, Alexis, and his family shelter and a way into the palace. He and Anya had also provided safe harbor and shelter to Willem's parents. He repaid some of that by announcing a celebration of a national holiday every year in honor of the senator's and Anya's roles in the crisis. They both smiled and nodded agreement to this honor.

It was Matt's and Lu-zan's turn. To them, Jon announced that from that day forward, Tyrea would establish an Intergalactic Police Training Facility on the planet in their honor. "I have nothing I can give you that would repay you for all you have done for me and our world." And he bowed low and long to honor them, which caused gasps of shock from everyone.

Last, he called Alexis forward. She blushed and moved to stop in front of him. Jon even got down on his knees to propose, which caused a lot of joyful laughter, although he was still unsure of her answer. He produced a small box from his pocket. Opening it, he took out a beautiful ring, which he had requested to be made by a local artisan. The artisan had worked around the clock so it would be ready.

Alexis couldn't take her eyes off it; it was so beautiful. He had it done with her birthstone, surrounded by a circle of very special stones the planet had produced for Jon. The stones were a color of the flower she loved and that blended wonderfully with the dark green emerald. Her eyes flicked up to Jon's face. *Oh, how I love this man,* she thought. *After everything we have gone through, he doesn't have to ask, but he will because that is who he is.*

He hesitated and took a deep breath. "Will you become my bride?"

"Oh yes, you silly man. I'm not letting you go anywhere," she whispered against his cheek. She thanked her lost love for reminding her to go with her heart and bring happiness to this man, who needed her as she needed him.

Jon slipped the ring on her finger, and she laughed and hugged him tightly. Jon gave her a long, deep kiss, which had the crowd howling and clapping in appreciation.

Jon stepped back from her. The crowd quieted down, excited to see what would happen next.

"All I have, I give to you, but I give you another title to go with the one of being my Queen Alexis. I also give you the title of Beloved." He bowed and held it until she pulled him up and kissed him once again to the wild cheering of the crowd.

The planet, Tyrea, watched and listened to all the celebration. It pulsed with contentment. It considered the humans that lived on its surface and knew that no matter what happened in the future, it was in excellent hands once again.

THE END

IN APPRECIATION

I couldn't have written this book without support from a lot of people. My readers, Malinda Mowrey, Connie Jenkins, Nancy Carney, Bob Farrington, Nicholas McKay, and Yancey Zimmer. Their input and encouragement were very helpful and much appreciated.

A heartfelt thank you to all the experts who guided me throughout this project. They are:

IngramSpark
ProWritingAid
SelfPubBookCovers
Integrative Ink

I really appreciated all your suggestions and comments and really feel like I am a better writer because of them. Thank you again.

CPSIA information can be obtained
at www.ICGtesting.com
Printed in the USA
BVHW091937111122
651745BV00008B/227